"I am not accustomed to an audience when I am making love to a lady . . ."

"Making love?" Gwenda gasped. "Dear heavens. Is that what you thought you were doing?"

His glare should have stopped her, but she could not let the poor man continue under such a delusion. "Oh, no, my dear Lord Treverly! I regret to tell you but you were doing everything absolutely wrong."

"Indeed, Miss Vickers?" Treverly said through clenched teeth.

"You should have been telling her something far more passionate than that you want a comfortable marriage. I'll also wager you never looked at Miss Carruthers when you were proposing, which is a great pity. You have the most handsome pair of eyes."

# BRIGHTON ROAD

## Susan Carroll

18/22

FAWCETT CREST • NEW YORK

A Fawcett Crest Book
Published by Ballantine Books
Copyright © 1988 by Susan Coppula

Library of Congress Catalog Card Number: 88-91163

ISBN 0-449-21390-0

Manufactured in the United States of America

First Edition: December 1988

To my good friend Linda Benjamin, for all her encouragement and support—this book is dedicated because very likely I will never write about a cowboy hero for her.

# Chapter 1

*Out of the mists he came—his windswept hair darker than a raven's wing, the pulse at the base of his throat throbbing with all the fury of the passionate Italian blood coursing through his veins. His scarlet-lined black cape swirled about his broad shoulders as he reached out his arms to her. Even though the castle ruins loomed behind him . . . even though its sinister shadow cast a blot upon the bright beauty of the moon itself, Gwenda felt safe as she hurled herself into his strong embrace . . . .*

Lost in the depths of her dream, Miss Gwenda Mary Vickers stirred upon the hard wooden settle in one of the White Hart's private parlors. Her short chestnut curls tumbled over her spencer, the folds of the rose-colored jacket scrunched up to form a pillow. Gwenda clasped to her bosom the heavy volume she had been attempting to read when she had fallen asleep. Hugging the book tenderly, she mumbled, "Oh, Roderigo. Roderigo, my love."

1

*His fingers, warm and rugged, crooked beneath her chin, forcing Gwenda to look up at him. Even as she did so, his features blurred, becoming obscured by the mists, but she sensed the full curve of his lips drawing closer to her own. . . .*

With a low groan, Gwenda rolled over, still clutching the book. Balanced precariously on the settle's edge, she moistened her lips in eager anticipation of her dream lover's kiss.

*His arms tightened about her. He pulled her closer, ever closer. She could feel the heat of his passion-drugged breath. His mouth was but a whisper away—*

*Thud!* Gwenda tumbled off the edge of the bench, landing hard upon the inn's polished wooden floor. The fall jarred her instantly awake. Gwenda sat bolt upright, shoving aside the heavy book that had somehow landed on top of her. Before she could so much as draw breath, she heard a low whine, and then a warm, rough tongue shot out, bathing the side of her face with affectionate concern.

"Down, Bertie," Gwenda commanded firmly, thrusting aside a large, lean dog, his glossy white coat spotted with black. She rubbed her bruised hip and blinked, trying to get her bearings.

Her gaze traveled upward along the coaching prints set upon stout oak walls, the fireplace swept clean of ash for the summer, the mantel laden with plates and mugs of gleaming copper and pewter. From outside the open window she could hear the clatter of iron-rimmed wheels and horses' hooves announcing more arrivals and departures from the ever-bustling inn yard.

Aye, she was in a private parlor of the White Hart. On the floor, to be precise. She had been cooling her heels here for the past three hours, ever since her carriage had snapped a brace a few miles outside the village of Godstone Green. The Hart's congenial landlord had very kindly offered her a book with which to pass the time. What was it now? Gwenda consulted the book's title page. Daniell's travelogue, *Views of the East*. Mr. Leatherbury's tastes in literature did not quite match her own. Small wonder that she had fallen asleep. Then she had begun to dream, only to fall off the high-backed settle just as . . .

Gwenda's green eyes darkened; her usually good-humored countenance tensed into a scowl. Fending off further attempts of her dog to console her, she heaved herself to her feet and plunked back down upon the settle.

"Damn!" she hissed. Her brother, the most holy Reverend Thorne Vickers, would have blanched with horror if he had heard her, but Spotted Bert was far more forgiving of her vagaries. The dog merely cocked his head to one side, arching a disreputable-looking ear that was much the worse from too many encounters with ill-mannered cats.

" 'Tis too provoking to be endured, Bertie," she said. Bert emitted a sympathetic bark and thrust his head upon her lap. Gwenda absently scratched him behind the ear. "I suppose I could have been in the throes of the most hideous

3

nightmare and I might have slumbered through the day undisturbed. But let me be caught up in the most delicious of dreamings and it never fails. I always wake up at the best part."

Her hand stilled, coming to rest upon the dog's head. She sighed, feeling bereft, as though she truly had been deprived of Count de Fiorelli's kiss. Although she could never bring his features clearly into focus, she knew his name well. The Italian nobleman had appeared in far too many of her fantasies, both sleeping and waking, besides having emerged as a character in many of the novels she wrote for Minerva Press. He might have borne a different name and title in both *The Mysteries of Montesadoria* and *The Dark Hand at Midnight*, but he was still, as ever, her Roderigo: brooding, passionate, and courageous.

Gwenda half smiled at her own nonsense, ignoring Spotted Bert as he nudged her hand with his cold nose, indicating his earnest desire that she resume the scratching. Although she had been writing Gothic tales of love and terror for the past three years, she would have stoutly denied she was a romantic. Nay, confirmed spinsters of one and twenty years were not supposed to give rein to flights of fancy. But there was always one foolish corner of her heart urging her to allow the bright colors of her imagination to splash over drab reality. Even now she was tempted to stretch back out upon the bench, shutting her eyes tight and seeking to recapture the dream. But experience had taught her that that never worked. It was possible to drift right back into nightmares, but never dreams. She would have to content herself with falling back upon her imagination.

But that was the difficulty. Her imagination never balked at conjuring what it would be like to have one's side skewered by a villain's sword, but that soul-searing kiss always eluded her. Despite two broken engagements, she had never experienced anything like it. Both Sir Jasper Pryor and Lord Marlon Lambert had been content to kiss her hand. Mayhap that was why she had never married either one of them.

Only once had she ever been kissed upon the mouth by a man, and that had been by her cousin Wilfred, the Christmastime she was fifteen. For a wager, her youngest brother, Jack, had made Wilfred do it by holding a sword to his back. With Wilfred's mouth so cold with fear, his hands clammy, his embrace had reminded Gwenda of a dead mackerel.

She could have *used* that dream kiss, Gwenda thought, to bring greater authenticity to the romantic scenes in her books. But there . . . She shrugged. She scarcely could spend the rest of the day moaning about it.

She reached down to pat Bert but found him gone. The animal's attention had been claimed by something he had spied through the window. His entire body taut with anticipation, a low, joyous growl erupted from Bert's throat. Gwenda recognized the sound only too well. It was a warning the dog reserved especially for his feline enemies.

"Bert!" she said, attempting to collar the dog. But it was too late. With a bunching of his powerful hindquarters, Spotted Bert cleared the sill and bounded outside. Gwenda reached the window in time to see a barking flash of black and white tearing between horses' legs in hot pursuit of a caterwauling fluff of gray.

She started to shout but immediately recognized the futility of the effort. Bert would not pay her the least heed. He would return when he was ready, to lament fresh scratches or with his tail wagging with victory at having forced his opponent to take refuge in a tree.

Gwenda scanned the crowded inn yard, hoping for some glimpse of her own coachman bringing her the welcome intelligence that the carriage would be ready soon for her to continue her trip to Brighton. Her family would be expecting her by five at the house Papa had rented in the Royal Crescent, and as matters now stood, it would be long after dark before she arrived, especially since she saw no sign of Fitch or her footman.

The inn yard appeared in more of a state of confusion than usual. A stage from London had just arrived, letting down its passengers for their twenty minutes of rest and refreshment. Just behind them an elderly gentleman was demanding a mug of ale and a change of horses for his post chaise. But most of the uproar stemmed from a large party that had just rattled into the yard, consisting of several carriages, a low perch phaeton, and some young bucks on horseback, all obviously traveling together on some sort of excursion. As the ladies were handed down from the coaches, waiters, ostlers, and postboys flew in all directions to provide the Hart's customary lightning service.

Even the host himself appeared harried. Mr. Leatherbury combined the mannerisms of a jolly country squire with a brisk efficiency in dealing with his guests. He mopped his cherubic countenance with a large kerchief as he bent his rotund frame into a bow to a tall man wearing a curly-brimmed beaver who alighted from the phaeton.

In the midst of such bustle, Gwenda did not doubt that the landlord had likely forgotten about the lady he had ushered into the private parlor hours before. She thought of sending her maid to make inquiries about the progress of repairs to her carriage, but as usual the pert French girl was nowhere to be found. Colette was likely off flirting with one of the handsome young waiters again.

Gwenda drew back from the window, eyeing with little enthusiasm the book that lay discarded upon the floor. If she didn't want to spend the rest of her afternoon absorbing more details about Indian mosques, mayhap she had best go to check on the carriage herself.

Returning to the settle, she retrieved the spencer that had served as her pillow and attempted to smooth out the rose velvet garment whose pile had been sadly crushed. She shrugged herself into the short-waisted jacket, then eased it over her traveling gown of dove-gray jaconet. She buttoned the frog enclosure, noting with a grimace how the spencer appeared to band tightly over the curve of her bosom, as all her apparel did.

7

Gwenda had oft heard herself described as "a handsome figure of a lady." She had always supposed that meant she had a chin a little too forthright for her to be considered beautiful, was too tall, and had full breasts. Her mother was forever reminding her not to hunch her shoulders forward. It was an old habit that had evolved from her youthful self-consciousness over being buxom when her friends yet appeared boyishly slender. Her mama had tried in vain to help Gwenda correct her posture. "A general's granddaughter," Prudence Vickers would remind her sternly, "should always maintain a proud military bearing." But Mama, not quite so amply endowed, had no notion of how self-conscious one felt. Those high-waisted clinging gowns that were now the fashion made Gwenda frequently feel like the figurehead on the prow of a ship.

Remembering her mother's admonishment, however, Gwenda did try to straighten a little. Without benefit of a mirror, she attempted to fluff some order into her wayward mass of curls, then headed for the door.

But she had not taken two steps when she realized she had forgotten something. Rather guiltily, she glanced down to where her stockinged toes peeked out from beneath the hem of her gown. It was another of her bad habits: forever discarding her shoes, then forgetting where she had put them.

In the sparsely furnished inn parlor, it took her little time to locate one of her Roman sandals by the settle. She sat down, then slipped her foot into the soft blue leather, quickly crisscrossing the lacing up her calf and tying it into a neat bow.

But the second sandal proved more elusive. She finally found it dropped behind the fireplace andirons as though someone had sought to hide it. She could well believe that *someone* had. Gwenda pursed her lips as she examined her footgear. The leather bore signs of many teeth markings, and the damp, frayed lacing was nigh chewed through. Now she knew how Spotted Bert had whiled away his time when she was napping.

"Blast you, Bertie," she muttered as she sank down on the settle, trying to figure out how she was going to wear the mangled sandal. She had hoped the dog had finally outgrown his penchant for gnawing on any unguarded shoes he could find. When the lacing broke off in her hand, she stifled an oath of vexation just as she heard the parlor door open behind her.

Gwenda hoped it would prove to be the errant Colette. Knowing that because of the settle's high back she could not be seen from the door, she started to peer around the wooden side to make her presence known. But instead of her maid it was the plump landlord who bustled in, saying, "Right this way, Lord Ravenel, and I shall have some refreshments sent in immediately."

To Gwenda's embarrassment, Mr. Leatherbury ushered in a strange gentleman who was so tall he had to duck to avoid banging his head on the oak lintel of the door. She shrank back behind the settle, quickly pulling her skirts down.

9

Thus composed, she prepared to call out and alert the host to his mistake: that this parlor was already occupied.

But before she could do so, she heard the man who had been addressed as Lord Ravenel say, "Refreshments will not be necessary. I only require the use of this room for but a few moments."

Gwenda heard Mr. Leatherbury's puzzled "Oh," then could almost imagine his shrug as he added, "Very good, my lord." He bustled out again, doubtless relieved to be able to attend to his more demanding guests.

As the door clicked shut, Gwenda realized she had been left alone with the stranger. Grimacing, she regarded with little relish the prospect of now limping out half-shod to announce her presence. But she was consumed with curiosity as well. Why on earth would someone desire the use of a private parlor for only a few moments? Before revealing herself, she cautiously risked a peek at Lord Ravenel, who stood just inside the door, briskly stripping off his gloves like a man marshaling himself for some grim and difficult task.

He certainly had to be one of the largest gentlemen she had ever seen, and all of him solid muscle, she would have wagered. From the heels of his gleaming Hessians to the crown of his glossy ebony hair, he stood well over six feet. A navy-blue frock coat molded perfectly a most unyielding set of broad shoulders. The cut of his immaculate cream-colored breeches and waistcoat were plain, with naught of the dandy about him; his neck was half strangled in a stiff collar and a cravat tied with mathematical precision. But the starched neckcloth appeared no more rigid than the cast of Ravenel's swarthy countenance. His features were rough hewn, from the square cut of his jaw to the harsh planes of his cheeks. Forbidding black eyebrows shadowed eyes as dark as the thick lashes framing them.

Not in the least shy or timid, Gwenda yet felt a trifle reluctant to point out to this formidable-looking man that the parlor was already occupied. Her hesitation proved costly. The next she knew, the door opened a second time. Her situation became more awkward when a waiter stood back to allow a lady to enter. Gwenda judged the lady to be not much older than herself, but far more elegantly gowned in corn-yellow satin, her fair ringlets wisping from beneath a poke bonnet. The waiter discreetly retired as the beautiful young lady regarded Ravenel through violet eyes gone wide with surprise.

"Lord Ravenel," she protested. "There was no need for you to bespeak a private parlor. We are all going to dine outside. The landlord has some tables arranged for our party beneath the trees. It will all be most charm—"

"I know that, Miss Carruthers," Ravenel said, sweeping her objections aside with a brusque motion of his hand. "But I wanted the favor of a few moments alone with you before we part."

Just the right amount of blush filtered into Miss Carruthers's cheeks to highlight her eyes. "That sounds most improper, my lord," she said,

11

dimpling with a tiny smile. "Mayhap I had best summon my aunt."

No more improper than her own position, Gwenda thought, mentally cursing the folly that had caused her to delay in speaking up. It would be dreadfully embarrassing for her to pop out now, but she had no desire to witness whatever sort of tryst was about to take place. And yet Ravenel's dark eyes looked more impatient than amorous. Gwenda crouched farther back on the settle, hoping that the lady might persuade him to leave, but his lordship appeared to be not the most persuadable sort of man.

"Of course I intend no impropriety," Ravenel said. "And your aunt would be very much in the way. Now sit down. Please."

Even when Ravenel added "please," it still sounded like a command. Gwenda heard the scrape of a chair and then a rustling of silk, which told her that Miss Carruthers had complied.

"Oh, blast!" Gwenda whispered to herself. Now what was she going to do?

Miss Carruthers said, "Surely, Lord Ravenel, whatever you have to say to me could wait until we meet again in Brighton."

"No, it cannot. I feel I have waited too long already."

Miss Carruthers's heavy sigh carried clearly to Gwenda's ears. Squirming at the plight in which she found herself, Gwenda eyed the open window through which Spotted Bert had vanished and wondered what her chances were of clambering through it unnoticed. But after risk-

12

ing another peek around the settle, she quickly abandoned any such notion. Miss Carruthers's chair was drawn up in the far corner of the room, closest to the door. Although Ravenel loomed over her, he did not look at the young lady. Rather, he seemed to be staring out the window, an absent expression in his eyes as he mustered his thoughts. Despite the discomforts of her situation, Gwenda could not help being caught up by the picture that two of them made, somewhat like the hero and heroine of her latest novel— Miss Carruthers, so angelically fair; Ravenel, so dangerously dark. Except that the backdrop was all wrong. Gwenda would have opted for walls of stone with rich Italian tapestries and velvet curtains of royal purple fringed in gold. Miss Carruthers's blond hair should have cascaded down her back instead of being arranged à la Sappho, and Gwenda would have rounded her eyes, gotten rid of that catlike slant. As for Ravenel, he would appear to better advantage in a crimson doublet, with a sword buckled at his waist. His hair should have flowed back from his brow in midnight waves rather than been cropped into the severe Brutus cut so popular among the gentlemen.

Linking his hands behind his back, Ravenel drew himself up to his full height. Mama, Gwenda thought, would greatly have approved of his lordship's posture. The man looked as though he had been born with a ramrod affixed to his spine. He said abruptly, "I see no reason to waste any more time, Miss Carruthers. I have your father's permission to address you, and I am sure you have been expecting me to do so."

Good heavens! Gwenda could scarcely credit her ears. The man could not possibly intend to deliver a proposal of marriage, not here at an inn.

But her own dismay was nothing compared to Miss Carruthers's. Dropping her manner of placid gentility, she half started from the chair, irritation and alarm chasing across her delicate features. "Oh . . . oh, no. I—I wasn't expecting— Please, Lord Ravenel. Desmond. 'Tis yet too soon."

Desmond! Gwenda stifled the desire to shriek. She was not so unreasonable as to expect to find men named Roderigo or Antonio outside the pages of her books, but *Desmond* . . . How could his parents have been so utterly unfeeling?

" 'Tis not too soon," Ravenel snapped. "I have received enough encouragement from you, Belinda, that I think I may make bold to speak what is in my mind."

In his mind? What about his heart? Gwenda thought. She realized she had been staring so long that, despite her concealment, she marveled that they did not feel her eyes upon them. Both Ravenel and Miss Carruthers appeared so caught up in their own drama that neither seemed to suspect that they were not alone.

All the same, Gwenda cautiously drew farther behind the settle. Resigning herself to the fact that she was now cornered until the end of this painful little scene, she eased into a more comfortable position as Ravenel launched into his proposal. He had a magnificent voice, deep and full-timbred. But his delivery—Gwenda winced. He might have been addressing a meeting of Parliament. She could almost picture his rigid stance, one hand resting upon the lapel of his jacket. He detailed quite logically and clearly for Miss Belinda Carruthers all of the advantages of becoming Lady Ravenel. These seemed to consist chiefly of estates in Leicestershire, a house in town, and an income of twenty thousand pounds a year. He was also prepared to generously overlook Miss Carruthers's own lack of fortune.

Gwenda shifted on the settle, having to bite her tongue to overcome the urge to interfere. Ravenel was doing it all wrong. Not that she was insistent that a man go down upon one knee. But at least he ought to clasp Miss Carruthers's hands between his own and forget all this rubbish about estates.

"In conclusion," his lordship said, "I believe our similarities of tastes and interests make for the likelihood of us achieving a most comfortable marriage."

Gwenda smothered a groan against her hand.

Ravenel added, almost as an afterthought, " 'Tis only for you, madam, to name the day that will make me the happiest of men."

A pause ensued at the end of his speech, which drew out to such lengths that Gwenda could not forbear sneaking another look even if it meant risking detection. Miss Carruthers appeared tormented with indecision, her pretty face not so much flustered as gone hard with calculation. The only thing Gwenda could liken the woman's expression to was when she saw her brother Jack contemplating some desperate gamble.

"No!" Miss Carruthers finally blurted out. "I—I mean yes, I cannot . . ." She flounced to her feet. "I mean I—I am deeply sensible of the honor you do me."

Not half as sensible of it as he was, Gwenda thought wryly as she noted Ravenel's brow furrowing with the weight of a heavy frown. Then she realized her interest in the situation was causing her to lean too far forward and pulled herself back.

"I beg your pardon," he said. "But am I to understand that you are refusing my offer?"

"No!" Belinda cried. "What—what I truly feel is that I cannot marry you . . . not—not at this time."

"My dear Belinda," he began again, but his growing irritation robbed the endearment of any effect. "Do you wish to marry me or not? A simple yes or no will suffice."

What a passionate attempt at persuasion that was, Gwenda thought, rolling her eyes. How could Miss Carruthers possibly resist!

"If you would only wait until I come to Brighton," Belinda faltered. "Just give me a little more time . . ."

"A little more time in Lord Smardon's company?" Ravenel said. "I am not a complete fool, Belinda. I am fully aware that the *friend* you intend to visit on the way to Brighton is the Earl of Smardon. You are hoping to marry him, are you not? That is why you will not return a round answer to my proposal."

"Oh, n-no. I don't mean to marry anyone." Belinda's voice dropped so low, Gwenda had to strain very hard in order to hear her. "There—there is another reason for my reluctance. You see, I was once engaged to a young officer, er, ah . . . Colonel Adams of the Tenth Cavalry. He—he died fighting in Spain. I fear I have not quite gotten over my Percival's death."

"'Once engaged'?" Ravenel echoed. "You never mentioned anything of the kind before."

With good reason, Gwenda thought cynically. There was a note of insincerity in Belinda's voice that made the whole thing sound like a hum.

"I hope I am not the sort of lady who goes about wearing her heart on her s-sleeve." Belinda's voice broke.

When Gwenda next peeked at the couple, she saw that Belinda's eyelashes batted, fighting back the tears that made her eyes sparkle like jewels. Appearing damned uncomfortable, Ravenel dredged up a linen handkerchief, which he thrust at her. Gwenda wondered why the young lady's distress roused no sympathy in her. Rather, she felt as though she had stumbled into the second act of a very bad melodrama.

"Thank you, Lord Ravenel," Belinda said, dabbing at her eyes with the linen. She gave a brave little sniff. "I am sure you understand now why I wish you to give me more time."

"But—" Ravenel began.

"Pray don't distress me by saying more just now. I will give you my answer in—in Brighton." Miss Carruthers at last managed to skirt past him. She bolted through the parlor door, fairly closing it in his face when he tried to follow.

Gwenda waited tensely for Ravenel's reaction. He did not look like the sort to slap his forehead or tear his hair and lament. For a moment he stared at the closed door, looking rather nonplussed. Then he scowled, his eyes seeming to grow darker and darker until Gwenda thought even the most black-hearted villain she had ever created would have thought twice about trifling with his lordship in his present mood. She half expected he would swear and drive his fist against the door panel.

But although his jaw set in a hard, angry line, Ravenel merely snatched up his gloves and put them on again with sharp, savage tugs. Gwenda held her breath for fear he might yet take a notion to walk farther into the parlor. When he reached for the door handle, she had to smother a sigh of relief. She sank back, congratulating herself on escaping undetected, when she heard a sharp bark. The next instant Bert jumped back through the window, his muddied paws skidding on the wooden floor.

With an inward groan, Gwenda flattened herself against the settle as Bert galloped over to where she sat. She shooed the dog frantically with her hand, hissing, "Go away, Bertie." But Spotted Bert was entirely impervious to such hints. He barked and wagged his tail as though he had not seen her for a twelvemonth, then assaulted her hand with rough, affectionate licks.

"What the deuce!" Gwenda heard Ravenel exclaim. With a sinking heart, she listened to the

18

sound of his boots striding across the room. She had not a chance to move so much as a muscle before his lordship was bending over the settle and peering directly into her face.

"H-hullo," she said with forced brightness as she struggled to fend off Bert.

Never had she seen a man look more thunderstruck. Ravenel's expression was exactly what she had been trying to achieve in her last book for Count Armatello when he saw the ghost of his murdered sister rise up before him.

Ravenel's astonishment quickly gave way, his face suffusing with a dull, angry red. Gwenda could see the storm brewing in those brilliant black eyes and hastily sought for words of explanation and apology, but before she could say another word, Bert began sniffing at Ravenel's sleeve.

Ever a sociable creature, her dog took a sudden, violent fancy to his lordship. His tongue lolling out, Bert leaped up, trying to lick Ravenel's chin. With a muttered oath, Ravenel tried to thrust aside the eager, panting animal.

"Oh, no! Bad dog. Heel, Bertie!" Gwenda cried.

But Bert never heeled. He continued to leap up as though determined to scale Ravenel, scraping his muddy paws clean upon the length of his lordship's immaculate cream-colored breeches.

"Down!" Ravenel said sternly, collaring Bert and forcing the animal back upon all fours. The dog whined and fidgeted while looking adoringly up at Ravenel.

Gwenda saw in Bert's intrusion a chance for her to escape from what promised to be a most unpleasant confrontation. She stood up, reaching for Bert's collar and said, "I do apologize for Bertie's behavior, sir. If you will permit me, I'll just be taking him—"

"Sit!" Ravenel thundered.

To Gwenda's mortification, she obeyed the command with more alacrity than the dog did. She plopped back down upon the bench. Spotted Bert gave in reluctantly, lowering his hindquarters to sit on her feet. To her astonishment, he remained seated even after Ravenel released his collar.

"That's absolutely amazing," Gwenda could not help exclaiming. "Bertie never listens to anyone."

"A trait that his mistress apparently doesn't share." With a look of disgust at his breeches, his lordship brushed at some of the mud stains with his gloved fingers.

Gwenda had the grace to blush. "I am so dreadfully sorry, Lord Ravenel. I did not mean to eavesdrop, but indeed I can explain why I did so."

He folded his arms across his chest. "I am all eagerness to hear your reason, madam."

Gwenda thought he looked far more eager to throttle her, but she continued in a rush, "You see, I was waiting in here while my carriage is being repaired, but the landlord forgot I had already claimed the use of the parlor and he—"

"And I daresay you experienced a sudden loss of voice that prevented you from speaking up."

"Everything happened so fast, and then—"

"And then you decided it would be far more

interesting to skulk behind the bench and listen."

Gwenda eyed him in frustration. "For someone who claims to be so eager to hear what I have to say, you have an annoying habit of interrupting me."

Ravenel silenced her with a lofty wave of his hand that Bert took for encouragement to assault his lordship again. After subduing the dog with another curt command, Ravenel fixed Gwenda with a stern eye. "Upon my word, madam. You should have had the delicate sensibility to make your presence known instead of spying upon a man like—like some chit of a schoolgirl."

Gwenda could have endured him railing or even swearing at her, as her brother Jack would have done, aye, and considered she deserved it. But when Ravenel lectured her in that stuffy manner, he reminded her of her odious brother Thorne.

"I am rather afraid I don't have any delicate sensibilities," she said.

"Nor scruples!"

"No, I am not overburdened with those, either," she agreed affably. "I do think you might have had more sense than to go about proposing to people in a public place like an inn. But, I daresay," Gwenda added, trying to be charitable, "that you were too worried that Lord Smi—Smardon, or whatever his name is, was going to steal a march on you with Miss Carruthers."

Ravenel's jaw dropped open in an outraged gasp. "Why, you—you impertinent little—"

"And it is only natural your lordship should be feeling a little surly—"

"Surly!" Gwenda thought he would choke on the word.

"Pray accept my heartiest condolences upon your recent disappointment," she concluded magnanimously.

"My recent disappointment is none of your affair." His voice started to rise, but with obvious effort he brought it back down again. "I do not even have the *honor* of your acquaintance, madam."

"Oh, so you don't. I am Miss Gwenda Mary Vickers." She swept to her feet and made him her best curtsy, but the regal effect was somewhat spoiled when she accidentally trod upon Bert's tail and he let out a reproachful yelp. As she bent down to soothe the dog, she realized Ravenel was regarding her with a mighty frown.

"Vickers? You are not—not by any chance one of the Bedfordshire Vickers?"

"Yes. Of Vickers Hall, just outside the village of Sawtree." She straightened, offering him her hand.

He didn't take it. A visible shudder coursed through him as he muttered, "Good Lord. One of the Sawtree Vickers. That explains everything."

Gwenda was not certain she liked his tone. She tipped her chin to a most belligerent angle. "And exactly what is that supposed to mean?"

"Nothing. Only that I have heard of your family before." Ravenel gave her one of those wary looks generally reserved for village idiots and the hopelessly insane. His eyes raked over her as though seeing her for the first time. Gwenda thought he dwelt on the curve of her breasts a little longer than he should have. She fought down a blush. Her Roderigo would have been far too high-minded for that.

Altogether she did not believe that his lordship was behaving with much gallantry, but she was willing to make allowances for a man who had been so recently crossed in love.

Once more she nobly tried to apologize for her intrusion. "Pray do not feel embarrassed over what I just witnessed, my lord. I assure you I am the soul of discretion."

His thick eyebrows arched up in sardonic fashion. " 'Tis difficult not to feel embarrassed. I am not accustomed to having an audience when I am making love to a lady."

"Making love?" Gwenda gasped. "Dear heavens! Is that what you thought you were doing?"

His glare should have stopped her, but she could not let the poor man continue under such a delusion. "Oh, no, my dear Lord Ravenel! I regret to tell you, but you were doing everything absolutely all wrong."

"Indeed, Miss Vickers?" Ravenel said through clenched teeth. "What a pity I hadn't realized you were present. I could have consulted you first."

"You should have been telling her something far more passionate than that you want a *comfortable* marriage. I'll also wager you never looked at Miss Carruthers when you were proposing, which is a great pity. You have a most handsome pair of eyes."

23

"Of all the arrant nonsense—" Ravenel began, turning an even deeper shade of red.

"There is still time for you to make amends. You could go after Miss Carruthers even now, take her in your arms and say—"

"Miss Vickers!" he snapped.

"No, I don't think she would like it if you called her by my name," Gwenda continued, undaunted. However, the black look Ravenel shot her did cause her to retreat a step. She could not help admiring the way his eyes smoldered when he was angry. Gwenda stared as if mesmerized into those raging dark depths, wondering rather breathlessly what he would do if he lost his temper. She had never been menaced by a man, as her hapless heroines were by the villains in her books. Obviously she could expect no help from Bert. The dog had rolled over onto his back and was shamelessly begging to have his stomach scratched.

With one powerful leap of her imagination, Gwenda conjured up images of everything from Ravenel's gloved fingers reaching for her throat to his restraining her ruthlessly against him. She felt vaguely disappointed when he merely drew himself up stiffly and said, "Since there is not the least likelihood we shall ever meet again, Miss Vickers, I have no intention of discussing my personal concerns with you any further. But, in future, let me advise you not to listen in on private conversations. Other men might be lacking in my considerable self-restraint."

"And let me advise you, my lord," Gwenda said, never able to refrain from having the last word, no matter what the risks, "that the next time you propose to a young lady, you find one that does not make you feel quite so *comfortable*."

Ravenel compressed his lips as though not trusting himself to reply. He spun on his heel and stalked over to wrench open the door. But this time he forgot to duck as he stomped across the threshold and slammed the top of his head against the door frame. The cracking sound was enough to make Gwenda wince in sympathy just hearing it. He reeled back, clutching his head, obviously seeing stars, the string of curses he wanted to utter trembling on his lips.

"Oh, damnation. Go ahead and say it," Gwenda urged impatiently. "I haven't any delicate sensibilities to offend, remember?"

She heard the indrawn hiss of his breath. His mouth clamped into a stubborn white line, but his snapping dark eyes did the cursing for him. Then he exited from the room with the most incredible forbearance Gwenda had ever witnessed in a man that furious. He didn't even slam the door behind him.

Gwenda let out her breath in a long sigh. "Well, of all the toplofty men I have ever met!" She bent down beside Bert, obliging him by scratching him at last and rendering the dog into a state of bliss with his eyes closed tight.

Gwenda tried to put the stuffy Lord Ravenel out of her head, but she could not help thinking about his lordship's broad shoulders, his raven's wing hair, and those marvelous flashing dark eyes so at odds with his rigid manner.

" 'Tis a great waste, Bertie," she said mournfully, shaking her head. "A great waste."

# Chapter 2

Desmond Arthur Gordon Treverly, the sixth Baron Ravenel, stormed down the inn corridor, seeking the White Hart's landlord. He fully intended to collar Leatherbury and inform the man that when his lordship requested a private parlor, by God, he expected it to be just that—*private*.

But he had to check his pace as he passed the coffee room and the stage passengers swarmed out. The twenty minutes allotted for their stopover had obviously come to an end, and if they did not resume their places, they would likely find themselves left behind. As this group tumbled out of the door, Ravenel glimpsed the apple-cheeked landlord about to rush in.

"Leatherbury," Ravenel shouted angrily, but the landlord paused only long enough to sketch a quick bow.

"I will be with you in a moment, your lordship," he said, huffing with great indignation. "There are some travelers who arrived on foot attempting to bespeak dinner in my kitchens and, I assure you, here at the Hart we do not cater to *that* sort of person."

Leatherbury's round face quivered with outrage, as though he placed walking in the same category as horse thieving. Then he bolted into the coffee room before Ravenel could say another word.

The baron considered it beneath his dignity to chase after the man. In any case, he was fair enough to concede that the affronts he had just received in the parlor were not precisely Leatherbury's fault. No, the blame must rest entirely with that extraordinary creature with the impudent brown curls and too candid green eyes.

"Making love? Is that what you thought you were doing?" The memory of Gwenda Mary Vickers's astonished gasp stung Ravenel worse than Belinda's not consenting to marry him. How dare that impertinent chit address him in such a manner! How dare she presume to eavesdrop, then to criticize him!

The floorboards trembled beneath Ravenel's feet as he stomped out through the inn's main door and into the bright sunlight. But the heat suffusing his face had naught to do with the warmth of the summer's day. Above his head, the inn's sign creaked, the white stag that had been the badge of Richard the Second authenticating the inn's claim that it had been built in the fourteenth century. Before him stretched the cobblestone street dotted with white-stone cottages baking in the afternoon sun. A line of fat geese waddled across the village green.

But both the bucolic charms of Godstone and

the ancient timber-frame inn were entirely lost on Ravenel as he continued to fume over his recent encounter with Miss Vickers.

Aye, as soon as he had heard her name, he had been well aware of what sort of behavior to expect. The Vickers family comprised the most notorious collection of lunatics to be found outside the confines of Bedlam. The insane exploits of Mad Jack Vickers were legend: shooting the currents beneath London Bridge, hiding inside a coffin to prove that he could survive being buried alive, balancing on one leg atop Lord Marlow's old coach horse. Mad Jack, the baron supposed, must be brother to the young lady he had just met. And as for the father! Ravenel grimaced. Never would he forget the time Lord Vickers had swept into the House of Lords clad in a Roman toga and delivered a speech more fit for Drury Lane than the august halls of Westminster. The mother, Lady Vickers, was said to be constantly besieging the Duke of Wellington with letters, telling him how he ought to be conducting the campaign against Napoleon.

Gwenda Vickers reportedly had some eccentricity, too, although at the moment Ravenel could not recollect what it was. Certainly a penchant for spying on total strangers must be numbered among her peculiarities. Doubtless she had a tongue that ran like a fiddlestick as well and would report his humiliation over half of England.

The prospect only aggravated Ravenel's ill humor. His gaze swept toward the distant spot where the rest of his traveling companions were seated upon benches beneath a large oak tree, a generous repast spread out on the table before them. But the baron felt no temptation to join them, not even when Miss Carruthers waved gaily and beckoned to him as though nothing had happened. He gave her a stiff nod, then turned away, still smarting from her recent rejection of him. Belinda had not said no precisely, but she wasn't exactly falling over herself to marry him, either. Although Ravenel would not have described himself as being heartbroken, his pride had been dealt a severe blow.

As he stalked around the side of the inn, heading for the stableyard, Gwenda Vickers's voice seemed to echo in his mind once more. ". . . you were doing everything absolutely all wrong . . . even now, you could go after Miss Carruthers, take her in your arms . . ."

"Bah!" Ravenel muttered under his breath. "What romantic piffle." Imagine offering such personal advice to a man she had never met before! Miss Vickers must be all about in her head, the same as the rest of her family. And yet he could not help mentally reviewing his wooing of Belinda, wondering if he had proceeded amiss. No. He shook his head. He could not concede that he had. He had conducted his courtship with the same seriousness and propriety he brought to all of his duties as Baron Ravenel. And in his thirty-second year, one of those duties was clearly to get himself a wife, then an heir.

Miss Carruthers had seemed such an ideal choice: a duke's granddaughter, a lady of breeding and refinement, intelligent and accomplished, not given to any wild whims of behavior—at least not until today.

Lost in his reflections, Ravenel drew back instinctively as the stage rattled past him away from the inn, the outside passengers clinging precariously to the top rail. So Belinda still mourned this—this Colonel Percival Adams who had died in Spain. Doubtless a cavalry officer with a fine pair of mustaches, and excessively dashing, which Ravenel was fully aware that he was not. "Sobersides"—that was the sobriquet bestowed upon him by the London wits.

The baron's jaw tensed. Not that he cared a jot what such society fribbles thought of him, nor that many wagers had been laid at White's betting that, despite all of Ravenel's assets, the fair Belinda would never have him. Likely she would choose his nearest rival, the Earl of Smardon, a golden-haired Corinthian of the first stare of elegance. A swaggering, muscled dolt with more brawn than brains, Ravenel thought scornfully, but his sneer quickly faded to a frown.

He fared ill by comparison to Smardon. The baron was well aware that he had not the least reason to be conceited over any of his personal attributes. He deplored the bronzed cast of his complexion that made him look more like some rascally buccaneer than a gentleman. But he also knew his own worth in terms of lands and the position he had to offer a lady. All during the London Season, Belinda had afforded him every encouragement, giving him reason to think his addresses would be acceptable to her until Lord

Smardon, the only other eligible bachelor whose holdings rivaled his, had appeared on the scene.

Although Ravenel was loath to admit it, Miss Vickers had been right when she had accused him of worrying that he would be cut out by Lord Smardon. His anxiety on that score had, mayhap, led him to commit the first breach of propriety in his life, proposing to Belinda at a common inn. And only see what humiliation that had brought him!

So unnecessary, too, for it seemed his rival was not Smardon but a soldier long dead. Odd. Never once had Belinda mentioned any such thing as being haunted by memories of a fiancé killed in the war. But, of course, a gentleman did not question the word of a lady, so Ravenel quelled all of his suspicions that Belinda was merely keeping him dangling, making a fool of him.

No, he had made up his mind to have Miss Carruthers for a wife, and have her he would. The Ravenels were excessively stubborn when it came to obtaining what they wanted. He would renew his addresses with more persistence when Belinda had finished junketing about with her aunt and arrived in Brighton.

This resolution took some of the edge off his anger and disappointment, but he still felt in no humor to make pleasant conversation over luncheon with his other traveling companions. Their destination was Tunbridge Wells; his was Brighton. He had only come with them thus far because of Belinda's presence in the party. But it would do the lady no harm to fret and fear she had displeased him.

Ravenel saw no reason why he should not continue on with his journey immediately. It was merely a question of collecting his elderly valet, Jarvis, from the coffee room and ordering his groom to have the phaeton brought round at once.

But his anger flared anew when he espied his new carriage drawn up before the stables, his prime pair of blooded bays pawing in the traces, completely unattended. With a low growl in his throat, which boded ill for the negligent Dalton, the baron hastened in that direction, barely avoiding being knocked down by a curricle departing from the inn yard.

Ignoring the driver's curses, Ravenel closed the distance between himself and his own rig. Not that he was that particular about the phaeton, but he took fierce pride in his cattle. He never trusted his bays to an ostler, no matter how high the inn's reputation. His groom, Dalton, was paid a handsome wage to see to the horses and make certain they were not so much as touched by any clumsy stable boy. The man had only been in Ravenel's employ a month, but he had given complete sastisfaction up until now. The baron trusted that Dalton would have some good excuse to offer for his neglect.

Unfortunately, when he located Dalton just inside one of the empty horse stalls, the groom did not seem of a frame of mind to offer any excuse. From the hazy look in his eyes, Dalton appeared incapable of even pronouncing his own name.

Backed against the side of the wooden stall, the short, wiry groom seemed about to go limp at the knees from the caresses of a petite, dark-haired wench with full, pouting red lips. Dalton stood scarcely over five feet high, and the girl was about his equal in height. Ravenel felt like a giant bearing down upon them.

The girl leaned forward until her bosom brushed against Dalton's thin chest. "Ooh, la, *monsieur* must be very brave to drive such wild horses."

Dalton blushed and stared down at the wench's clinging bodice front. " 'Tis really nothing, miss. 'Tis naught like 'is lordship owns one o' them 'igh-perch phaetons the sporting gentlemen drive. Something of a slow-top 'is lordship is."

As the girl giggled, Ravenel felt his cheeks begin to burn.

"The—the slow-top?" she repeated. "*Ça, c'est drôle. Monsieur* is so clever."

"So clever," Ravenel bit out, startling the couple into leaping apart, "I hope *monsieur* has no difficulty in finding himself a new position."

"Lord R-Ravenel." Dalton's eyes grew wide with guilt and dismay. He started to stammer out an apology, but the baron had already turned to stride out of the stables. Dalton followed after him, whining excuses.

Ravenel, although an exacting master, was usually most generous about giving erring servants a fair hearing and a second chance. But he felt he had borne enough insults this day. By God, he was not going to start tolerating insolence from his own hirelings.

Although it nigh killed him to do so, he ordered one of the ostlers to see to his bays. He cut off Dalton's blistering protest by drawing forth his purse and stuffing some pound notes into the groom's leathery hand.

"Your wages, sir," Ravenel said, eyeing the groom in a fierce manner that had cowed men far braver and more importunate than Dalton. "You may keep the boots, but, of course, you will return the livery."

"Aye, my lord," the groom said sullenly, scuffing his toe in the dirt.

The baron thrust a few more coins at the man. "And here is a little extra to cover your expenses back to London. I will even furnish a reference as to your skill in handling horses, but as to your reliability . . ."

He left the sentence incomplete, his scornful tone making it clear what he thought. Although Dalton pocketed the money, he did not trouble himself to conceal a look of resentment.

Ravenel dismissed the man's lowering expression with as much contempt as he did Dalton himself. Heading back toward the inn, he nearly collided with the cause of this recent trouble. The French girl deliberately thrust herself into his path, her heavy perfume filling his nostrils even above the odors of the stableyard.

Ravenel's nose crinkled with distaste. He by far preferred the smell of his horses. When the girl fluttered her lashes, showing every sign of being prepared to take up with him where she had left off with Dalton, his lordship gave her a wide berth.

As the baron stomped toward the inn door, he could only wonder at what was happening to the White Hart. Once the most respectable of hostelries, today the place was absolutely crawling with brazen females. Not that he was so unjust as to classify a lady such as Miss Vickers with the likes of that French doxy. But both women had managed to embarrass him in the short span of an hour and Ravenel looked forward to the prospect of never setting eyes on either again. He would round up Jarvis at once and be gone from this infernal place.

Despite the bustling atmosphere of the White Hart's coffee room, the waiters yet found time to pay Sebastian Jarvis the same amount of deference as he would have received at home. As the baron's eldest and most trusted servant, he was accorded a respect little short of that shown the master, a respect that his presence seemed to command wherever he went.

He was a distinguished-looking old gentleman with flowing white hair and keen blue eyes that no amount of years could dim. The lines upon his profile were finely stitched as though Time had become a seamstress, her needle gently fashioning an age-worn face mended with dignity. Jarvis bore more countenance than did most dukes who traced their ancestry back to the time of the Conqueror.

"More rum and milk, sir?" The young waiter hovered respectfully at Jarvis's elbow, ever ready to refill his mug.

"No, thank you, lad," Jarvis replied in his soft, courteous voice. Indeed he was not sure he should have had the first one. He had hoped the toddy might soothe the ache behind his eyes. What did ladies do when they got the megrims? Jarvis would have been mortified to ask.

When another waiter hustled forward to set a sizzling beefsteak before him, Jarvis regarded his meal with little appetite. He could not believe he had another of those wretched headaches.

But it seemed he acquired one every time he rode out in the hot sun with Master Desmond in the open carriage. Jarvis passed his hand across his brow with a small sigh. And to think of the way he used to ride on horseback all day, accompanying the present baron's grandfather in the most blistering summer weather. He stared mournfully into his empty cup.

"You're getting a little long in the tooth, Jarvis old man," he murmured. Aye, so he had been doing, these past ten years and more. His wry smile was reflected back at him in the cup's bottom.

But this time his discomfort was not entirely due to the heat of the day. Fretting over his young gentleman had done little to ease the steady throb behind Jarvis's temples. There was little about Master Desmond that he didn't know. Hadn't he acted as valet to the lad ever since he had been left an orphan at the tender age of nine, when typhus carried off the late Lord and Lady Ravenel? He was fully aware of all of his lordship's moods and therefore knew perfectly well why Master Des had disappeared into a private parlor and that Miss Carruthers hard after him. He ought to be wishing his young master every success and yet ... Jarvis heaved a heavy sigh. There was something about that Miss Carruthers, something cold and sly that kept Jarvis hoping the match would not come off, despite his master's wishes. The lady simply did not seem right for his Master Des.

But when Jarvis had ventured to utter even the slightest criticism of the lady, his lordship had flown up into the boughs. So, despite the familiarity that his long acquaintance with Master Desmond gave him, Jarvis had been wise enough not to offer any more unsolicited opinions, but that did not prevent him from continuing to worry.

When Ravenel finally made his appearance in the coffee room, Jarvis anxiously scanned his lordship's countenance for some sign that his fears had come to pass: Master Desmond was now engaged to Miss Carruthers.

But the baron's heavy brows were drawn together like a thundercloud hovering over the stormy darkness of his eyes. His mouth was set into a hard line. It would be obvious even to those who did not know Master Desmond well that something had happened to vex his lordship.

She must have refused him, Jarvis thought. Intermixed with his relief was a perverse anger at the lady who could thus have the bad taste to reject his fine young gentleman.

As Lord Ravenel strode toward his table, Jarvis pushed back his chair in order to rise. His lordship placed a restraining hand upon his shoulder. "Sit, Jarvis, and finish your meal."

Ravenel flung himself into the chair next to him and sent one of the waiters to fetch him a glass of ale. While he waited for it to be served, he drummed his fingers impatiently on the table. "As soon as you have finished eating, we'll be off."

"Very good, Master Des—" Jarvis broke off. Even after all these years, he sometimes forgot to call his gentleman by his proper title. "Very good, my lord," he amended.

While he picked at his beefsteak, he covertly studied the baron, hating the unhappy frown that carved deep ridges into Ravenel's brow. His lordship stared moodily out the window. Beyond the latticed panes, Jarvis could see the party of the baron's friends yet making merry beneath the oak tree, Miss Carruthers the merriest among them.

His master spent too much of his life peering out windows, Jarvis thought sadly. He was suddenly haunted by the memory of a much younger Master Desmond, trying conscientiously to grapple with learning to manage a vast estate, all the while stealing wistful glances to where his cousins played cricket upon Ravenel's lawn.

Jarvis coughed softly into his napkin and cleared his throat. "I—I could not help noticing, my lord," he said diffidently. "Am—am I not to wish you joy?"

"No, I am afraid not, Jarvis," Ravenel said, his frown deepening. He took a large pull from his mug of ale, then wiped his lips with a napkin, looking as though the brew had left a sour taste in his mouth.

"Never you mind it, Master Des," Jarvis said, just as he had done so many times before when his lordship's odious cousins had refused to include him in one of their escapades. He added, "There is many a young lady who would consider herself fortunate if you—"

"I doubt that," Ravenel said with such a bitter twist to his lips that it struck up a dull ache in Jarvis's heart. "In any event, I have not given up on Miss Carruthers yet."

"Then you mean to go with the others to Tunbridge Wells after all," Jarvis said. Despite the pain in his head and his uncertainty that his master's pursuit of Miss Carruthers was the best thing, he brightened. His master did not enjoy himself in the company of other young people half enough.

But Jarvis's hope was quickly dashed. "No, I am still going straight on to Brighton. I told you that my man of business is going to meet me there."

"So you did, my lord," Jarvis said, crestfallen. Business, 'twas always business with Master Des. His lordship had been drilled with a sense of responsibility far too early in life, with never a chance to enjoy all the follies of youth.

"Miss Carruthers will be in Brighton herself within a sennight." Ravenel frowned again as though the prospect did not entirely give him pleasure. He startled Jarvis by asking him abruptly, "Have—have you ever proposed to a lady?"

"Me, my lord? Good gracious, no."

The baron looked rather disappointed. "Then I suppose you have not the least notion how to go about it."

Regretfully, Jarvis did not. An inveterate old

bachelor, it distressed him to feel he could be of so little use to his master on this score. After much thought, he ventured, "I suppose the direct approach would be the best. Put the question plain and proper."

His answer seemed to please Master Desmond. "That's what I thought, too," Ravenel said, nodding his head in satisfaction as though somehow vindicated.

"Aye, my lord," Jarvis continued. "If the young lady cares at all about you, she should not need much by way of persuasion."

The rest of his answer did not seem to delight Master Desmond as much. As his lordship became lost in another brown study, Jarvis bit back the urge to say, Forget that blond minx, Master Des. Miss Carruthers was such a cold sort of beauty with her pale-colored hair and winter-blue eyes. Master Desmond needed a lady with all the riot and warmth of springtime. But that was not the sort of poetic sentiment a dignified valet should be expressing, not even if he had served the family through three generations.

Ravenel tossed off the last of his ale and then rose with his characteristic abruptness. "Well, Jarvis, if you are done harassing that unfortunate beefsteak, we'd best be off. I should like to make Brighton well before dark, especially since we will be traveling alone. I have dismissed Dalton."

Over the years Jarvis had trained himself not to show surprise. "Indeed, sir?" was all he said.

"Yes, the fellow was too impudent by half."

Although Jarvis heartily agreed with him, he

yet felt a little disturbed by the tidings. It was not like Master Desmond to act so quickly and out of hand. He should not like to think his lordship's recent disappointment was starting to cloud his judgment.

He stood up to follow Ravenel from the coffee room, not looking forward to an afternoon of the hot sun beating down upon his already aching head. But he had barely taken a step when the floor seem to rock beneath his feet, the paneled walls of the coffee room spinning before his eyes.

"Jarvis!"

He caught a flash of Ravenel's face gone pale with concern. His lordship's strong arm eased Jarvis back into his chair.

After a few moments with his eyes closed, the world around him resumed its normal steady balance. " 'Tis—'tis nothing, my lord," he said. "Except a drop too much rum."

"The devil it is! The heat has been bothering you again and you never said a word to me."

"N-nonsense. Fit as a fiddle, I assure you." Jarvis would have attempted to rise again, but Ravenel refused to let him.

"Well, that settles it. We shall spend the night here and go on to Brighton in the morning."

"Never, my lord," Jarvis quavered with indignation. "Certainly not on my account."

"To own the truth, I am feeling rather exhausted myself."

Jarvis knew a plumper when he heard one. He could not remember the day his lordship had ever admitted to feeling tired. Besides, Master Des had a trick of not quite meeting one's eye when he was being less than truthful. However, before Jarvis could protest, the baron rushed on, "Besides, I fear one of the bays might be straining a fetlock. That was why I dismissed Dalton—for neglect. No, I think we should all do better for an afternoon's rest."

Jarvis grumbled, "Well, the bit about the horse is a far better tale than that nonsense about you being fatigued, my lord—"

"Good. I am glad you liked it." Ravenel flashed one of his rare smiles. "You wait here a moment. I shall bespeak rooms for us and see to it that the bays are properly stabled."

"Master Desmond!" Jarvis made one last attempt to protest, but the baron was already striding from the room. He knew there would be no dissuading his master now. Obstinate he was, once he got a notion in his head, like all the Ravenels before him.

Jarvis's shoulders slumped with dejection. What a worthless old stump he was, delaying Master Desmond this way. His lordship needed one of those smart young valets who could keep pace with him and rig him out in dashing style, make that Miss Carruthers suffer a few pangs of regret over trifling with Master Des's feelings.

The bleakness of Jarvis's reflections increased when he later peered through the coffee-room window and saw that the rest of Master Desmond's friends were departing for their carriages. Although his lordship was there to bid farewell to Miss Carruthers, she was too busy flirting with one of the other young bucks to even offer her hand to be kissed. When the coaches rattled away down the street, followed by the young men, laughing and shouting, on horseback, all gaiety seemed to have fled with them. Ravenel was left standing in the shade of the oak tree, his hand raised in a gesture of farewell that no one appeared to notice. Alone, Jarvis thought with a heavy heart. As ever, Master Desmond was alone.

As the sun set over Godstone's red-tiled roofs, Ravenel watched Jarvis light the candles in his bedchamber. The room was comfortable enough as inn rooms went, with a large four-poster bed, although Ravenel could have done without the lavender scented sheets.

For about the dozenth time, the baron started to pace, then checked himself, struggling not to reveal his restlessness to Jarvis. He could have been in Brighton by this time, he thought, then was immediately ashamed of himself. Nay, what did one more day matter? He had already been inconsiderate enough, not noticing that the heat had been making Jarvis ill. The valet had been part of the fabric of his life for as long as Ravenel could remember, as much a solid, comforting presence as the baron's beloved home. He kept forgetting that the old man must be well into his seventies.

Studying the elderly servant's face as he laid out the baron's night things, Ravenel mentally applauded his decision to break the journey. Jarvis was looking much better for an afternoon spent resting within the cool confines of the inn.

The pinched whiteness about his mouth and the lines of strain feathering the corners of his eyes had been eased. The delay in his traveling plans was a small price to pay, Ravenel reflected, to see Jarvis looking much more the thing again. After a good night's sleep, the elderly valet should be restored to his invincible, stately self.

Although he did not feel in the least tired, Ravenel feigned a yawn. "Well, I think I shall be turning in early, Jarvis, and I suggest you do the same. I mean to be off at cock's crow tomorrow."

"Very good, my lord. I'll just polish your Hessians and then—"

But the baron moved more quickly than the valet and snatched up the soiled leather footgear before Jarvis could reach them.

"There is no need for you to bother about that. I will simply send them belowstairs to the boots. That is what those fellows are hired for after all."

"The boots, my lord?" Jarvis gasped, his features settling into an expression of dignified horror. "You—you would trust your Hessians to a common servant at an inn?"

"Why not? You know I am no dandy, Jarvis. It makes no odds to me whether I can see my face reflected back in a bit of leather."

"But, my lord—"

"And," Ravenel continued, his eyes skating away from any direct contact with his valet's outraged blue ones, " 'tis now the fashion to have one's footwear sent down to be polished by the boots."

It was a damned clumsy lie and Ravenel

greatly feared he was wreaking havoc with Jarvis's pride, but he would not have the old man sitting up to polish the Hessians when he should be in bed. The baron strode firmly to the door. Ravenel flung it open, preparing to summon one of the inn servants.

Instead of one of the maids, he saw the lanky figure of the boots himself just a few doors down the inn corridor. The boots was squatting down to pat the head of a familiar black and white dog, and standing next to him was an all-too-familiar dark-haired lady.

Good lord, Ravenel thought, freezing on the threshold of his chamber. That Vickers woman was still running tame at the White Hart. He had assumed her carriage had been repaired and she had departed hours ago.

At the present moment, she was thanking the boots for returning her dog. "I am pleased to hear that you think Bertie such a friendly creature. Indeed, he is most sociable, but I ought to warn you. I fear he has not been bearing you company out of entirely disinterested motives."

The boots appeared as bewildered by this strange statement as Ravenel himself, overhearing it. But he was not going to risk another encounter with Gwenda Vickers merely to satisfy his curiosity as to what she was talking about. He attempted to step back quietly and close the door.

But it was too late. The incorrigible Bertie had already spotted him. With a joyous bark, the animal came loping toward him as though Ravenel were his long-lost master. The baron braced himself for the assault, but handicapped as he was by the Hessians still clutched under his arm, he had to endure several licks sweeping from the tip of his chin up to the bridge of his nose before he could collar the dog.

"Heel, you infernal hound!" he said as Gwenda hastened over to intervene. "Miss Vickers, have you no control over this wretched animal?"

"None whatsoever, I'm afraid," she said cheerfully. Ravenel thought she might at least appear a little uncomfortable to encounter him again, considering the circumstances of their last meeting. But far from appearing disconcerted, she seemed absolutely delighted to see him.

"Lord Ravenel. This *is* splendid," she said. "I thought you had gone. I was going to post it to you, but now I shan't have to. Just wait here. I won't be a second."

Before the baron could protest or even inquire as to what the deuce *it* was, Miss Vickers spun about and raced off down the corridor. She was already whisking into one of the rooms when it occurred to him that she had left him to struggle with her dog.

"Miss Vickers," Ravenel fumed as her bedchamber door clicked shut with an ominous finality. Bertie was showing a strong desire to bolt inside Ravenel's own room and make Jarvis's acquaintance.

"Oh, no, you don't," he muttered, although it took a great deal of his strength to dissuade the friendly animal. He managed to ram his Hessians into the hands of the boots, who had stood watching the entire scene with a huge grin on his face.

"Would yer lordship be needing a bit of a hand?" the boots asked.

"No!" Ravenel said, having succeeded in thrusting Bertie back along the corridor. "You just look after my Hessians. I'll be wanting them first thing in the morning." And to Bertie he commanded, "And you! Get along. Follow your mistress."

Bertie whined. Wagging his tail, he gazed soulfully at the baron. Hardening his heart against the dog's mournful look, Ravenel retreated into his room and slammed the door. He released his breath in a gusty sigh and proceeded to straighten his cravat, which had gone askew in the struggle with the dog.

He turned to meet Jarvis's questioning look. "My lord, whatever is—"

But the elderly valet's question was cut off by the sound of a light rapping on the door. The dog couldn't knock. Ravenel assumed it had to be *her*.

He grimaced and closed his eyes. Would Jarvis think he had run completely mad if he told the valet to pretend that he wasn't here? No, it wouldn't serve. Nor could he permit his venerable valet to open that door and be flattened by the exuberant Bertie.

"Never mind, Jarvis," Ravenel said, moving with a quickness that belied his weary tone. "I'll deal with this."

Cautiously he inched open the door, but there was no sign of the dog, only Miss Vickers. She appeared completely unruffled, as though it was the most natural thing in the word for an unescorted lady to knock at the chamber door of a strange gentleman.

Balancing three slender leather-bound volumes in her hand, she said reproachfully, "Lord Ravenel. You didn't wait."

Before he could reply to this accusation, she added, "Have you got Bertie in there with you?"

"No, I most certainly have not!" Ravenel snapped.

"Blast! Then I suppose he has gone following the boots again." She added darkly, "As if I didn't know what mischief that dog is plotting." She glowered in the direction that Bertie had presumably disappeared.

The baron shifted impatiently. "Miss Vickers, was there something you wanted of me?" he asked in accents of the most awful civility.

"Oh, yes. Yes, there was." His question seemed to snap her attention back to himself. Ravenel found himself staring into her wide green eyes. He noted that they were not precisely green. They had flecks of gold in them. Or was it that she had golden eyes with flecks of jade? 'Twas difficult to tell. Her eyes seemed to have a trick of changing according to the lighting and her mood. Also, she had the most absurdly long dark eyelashes he had ever seen.

". . . and I treated you very badly this afternoon."

With a start, Ravenel realized Miss Vickers was apologizing to him.

"I had no right to be eavesdropping and

thrusting myself into the midst of your affairs. It was abominably rude of me—"

"Miss Vickers, please!" The baron held up one hand to stem this breathless flow of words. "I think the less said of this painful matter, the better. I have no desire except to forget it ever happened."

"But I cannot forget. Not until I make you some amends. I have a gift for you and I hope you will accept it."

A gift! Ravenel bit back a shocked exclamation. Did this young lady have any notions of propriety? "Really, Miss Vickers," he said. "I don't think that you should—"

"Oh, please," she begged, extending the stack of books to him with a wistful smile. Ravenel would not have said Gwenda Mary Vickers was a beauty, but he was forced to admit that she had an unusually appealing smile. It was not coy or of a forced politeness; it was warm and genuine.

He shuffled his feet uncomfortably. "Well, I . . ."

His hesitation was all the encouragement she needed to eagerly thrust the books into his hands. With some trepidation, he stole a glance at the title. *The Dark Hand at Midnight* in Three Volumes, by G. M. Vickers. Good God! Ravenel stifled a groan. Now he remembered Miss Vickers's peculiarity. She wrote those blasted Minerva Press novels, which were all about swooning women, family curses, men dashing about with swords making cakes of themselves, and ghosts and villains popping out of the wainscoting.

As the baron sought for some civil way to toss

*The Dark Hand* right back at Miss Vickers, he felt something brush against his sleeve and was startled to see Jarvis attempting to peek past him into the corridor. Never in his life had Ravenel known his valet to display such a vulgar emotion as curiosity.

Gwenda Vickers dipped into a curtsy and beamed at Jarvis. "Good evening, sir," she said. "I assume you must be Lord Ravenel's uncle?"

"Why, no, miss."

"This is my valet," the baron filled in drily. "Jarvis."

"Oh!" Miss Vickers did not look in the least disturbed by her mistake. "How astonishing, for there is such a remarkable resemblance between you. Although not the same color, you both have remarkably handsome eyes."

It was the second time Miss Vickers had made that idiotic remark about his eyes being handsome, Ravenel thought irritably. It was high time this awkward and exceedingly improper interview drew to a close. He supposed the quickest way to do that was to graciously accept the wretched book. He shoved the volumes at Jarvis and then turned to thank Miss Vickers in his most rigid manner.

"Not at all," she said. "I only hope you enjoy the book. I have marked one particular passage for you in the second volume. It is where Antonio, Count Delvadoro, passionately proposes marriage to Lady Emeraude."

"Miss Vickers!"

The lady seemed totally oblivious to his warning growl.

"I don't mean to press the point," Gwenda said, "but I really do feel you are in want of just a few suggestions."

"Not from you!" Ravenel pressed his lips together, waiting until he felt his rising temper was more under control before he continued. "I beg your pardon, Miss Vickers, but fiction is one thing, reality quite another."

"Pooh! Why should it be?"

"Why should it—" Ravenel choked. Then he realized his mistake. He was trying to reason with Miss Vickers as though she were a sane person and not a Vickers at all. He sighed. "I shall try to find time to read the book, Miss Vickers. Now you really should not keep standing about in a drafty inn corridor."

"And if you will most particularly note that one passage—"

"Yes, yes. Good night, Miss Vickers." He eased the door closed, hearing her muted "Good night, Lord Ravenel" through the heavy portal.

He stood by the door, listening for the sounds of her retreating down the corridor. He frowned. A lady of quality should not be wandering about alone at an inn like that. For all of Miss Vickers's unusually forward behavior, Ravenel sensed a certain childlike innocence about her. The lady was clearly not up to snuff and required some sort of a keeper.

In spite of a voice sternly reminding him that it was none of his concern, the baron could not refrain from inching the door open a crack and peeking out to make sure she had gone safely back to her room.

51

He saw Miss Vickers about to cross her own threshold when her head snapped toward the end of the hallway where the stairs led up from below.

"Colette!" Miss Vickers said in a tone of mild exasperation. "I was wondering where you had gotten to this time."

Colette. So Miss Vickers did at least have some sort of a female traveling companion, Ravenel thought with an inexplicable sense of relief. But his relief quickly changed to dismay when he saw the pert female who approached Miss Vickers. Damnation! It was that French doxy he had caught practicing her seductive wiles upon Dalton in the stables.

"Pardon, *mademoiselle*," Colette said. "I was but fetching your warm milk from the kitchens."

She bobbed an insolent curtsy and handed the glass to Miss Vickers. Something in the Frenchwoman's expression as she followed Miss Vickers into her bedchamber disturbed Ravenel. Colette's sinister smile would have done credit to a Lucrezia Borgia.

The chit was obviously a person of no character, a scheming lightskirt. Miss Vickers ought to be warned and— And what the deuce was he thinking of?

The baron closed his door, appalled by his own fanciful notions. He was permitting his imaginings to run away with him on the basis of witnessing one sly smirk, harboring thoughts more worthy of the whimsical Miss Vickers than of his own orderly mind. Ravenel passed a hand over his brow, wondering if lunacy could possibly be contagious.

In any event, the lady and her maid were none of his affair. He was trying to curtail all future acquaintance with Miss Vickers, not entangle himself further with the lady.

*The Dark Hand at Midnight*, indeed, he thought contemptuously. He would make sure to instruct Jarvis that those volumes should be conveniently forgotten when they left the White Hart tomorrow.

But when Ravenel turned, he was appalled to discover that Jarvis—that most correct and sensible of gentlemen's gentlemen—had donned his spectacles and was already deeply engrossed in Volume One.

# Chapter 3

The morning sun streamed through the windows of Gwenda's room, patching the bed with squares of light. She could feel the warmth upon her face, but she could not seem to force her eyes open to confront the breaking of day. Nor did her limbs seem to want to move, either. She felt as though she had been swathed in cotton batting from head to toe with some of the fluffy whiteness actually stuffed inside her head. A low groan escaped her lips, some part of her mind registering the fact that she had just passed a very strange night. It was not natural for her to sleep so heavily, so deeply without dreams. She always had some sort of dreams.

With great effort, she at last managed to shift her legs from beneath the coverlet. Something warm and moist was licking the soles of her feet. Gwenda struggled up onto one elbow and regarded the black and white blur at the foot of her bed through bleary eyes.

"Bertie," she tried to call but scarcely recognized her own voice. When had her tongue gotten to be so thick?

The dog stretched, then ambled along the length of the bed. She patted him, coming slowly more awake as he nuzzled her.

"That'll do, Bertie." She chuckled when his rough tongue tickled her ear. She caught the dog's head firmly between her hands and mumbled, "I trust you will be a good dog today and behave more civilly if we chance to meet Lord Ravenel again."

Bertie gave a sharp bark as though he understood.

She yawned, scratching his ear. "Aye, like all rogues, you are most quick with your promises, sir."

She knew full well Bertie would conduct himself as outrageously as he always did. Not that it mattered. She supposed there was little likelihood they would see Lord Ravenel again. Even if he hadn't gone, she sensed that his lordship would dodge her company. Why could she simply not leave him alone? It was one of her own principles to avoid rigorously any gentleman with too much starch in his collar. She had too oft found it denoted a most humorless outlook on life.

She might certainly have put Ravenel down as the stuffy lord he appeared to be, striking eyes or no, if she had not chanced to be walking toward the front of the inn at a particular moment yesterday afternoon. It was then that she had seen Ravenel as he stood and waved good-bye to Miss Carruthers. He must be more in love with the lady than Gwenda had at first supposed, for he had appeared not so much high in the instep as unhappy and vulnerable. Gwenda's intuition told her that Lord Ravenel was a lonely man, and she could not bear to see anyone left lonely. But what could she do to alter Ravenel's case? He was obviously not the sort of man to accept anyone's advice.

"I doubt my interference did any good at all, Bertie," Gwenda murmured to her dog. "Most likely he used my book to light the fire as soon as I was gone, and the next time he woos Miss Carruthers or any other lady, he'll make the same mistakes all over again."

Gwenda sighed, then shrugged. At least she had the satisfaction of knowing she had tried. She swung her legs over the side of the bed. Through eyes yet dulled with sleep, she squinted at the small china clock ticking on the mantel. Good heavens! Five minutes after the hour of ten. If that time were correct, then the morning was more advanced than she had at first supposed. She was not ordinarily a late sleeper.

"Colette?" Gwenda called, stretching her arms over her head and suppressing another yawn. She spoke more sharply when she received no answer. "Colette!"

There was still no response from the adjoining chamber.

"Rot that girl. Sleeping in again and deaf as a post besides. I tried to tell Mama she would never do." Grumbling, Gwenda pushed herself to her feet and was surprised to feel that her legs were a little wobbly. Even the swat of Bertie's tail against her calves seemed enough to unsteady her. She staggered to the white porcelain wash-basin. She strained to lift the heavy pitcher and splash a small quantity of water into the bowl.

Taking a deep breath, she heroically dashed some of the cold water onto her face. Although she gasped with the shock, it felt good, setting all her pores a-tingle, and driving off the last wisps of fog that clouded her brain. As she reached for a linen towel to dry herself, her gaze fell on a soiled glass left on the nightstand.

Her nose crinkled at the curdled remnants of the milk she had drunk last night. Beastly stuff. She would not have bothered with it if Colette had not pestered her so. The milk had had the most peculiar undertaste. She must remember to speak to Mr. Leatherbury about it.

But the first order of business was to rouse Colette to help her dress, then make inquiries as to whether that dratted coach brace had been mended.

Gwenda shuffled barefoot across the carpet to the door of the small chamber that adjoined hers and rapped loudly. "Colette!" This time she did not wait for any response before unceremoniously shoving the door open. The sight that met Gwenda's eyes momentarily drove all thoughts of her errant maid from her head. She gave a tiny gasp and stood frozen in the door frame.

Her portmanteau, which had been arranged so neatly along the wall of Colette's room, were now tumbled about the room. The lids were flung open, the trunks empty except for a few trifling articles of clothing strewn over the floor.

It took Gwenda's stunned senses a few moments to recover before her mind assimilated the truth.

"Why, I . . . I've been robbed," she whispered, a sick feeling striking in the pit of her stomach. But how and when? She could not forbear a nervous glance about her as though she might find the thief yet lurking behind the curtains or beneath the bed.

No, she was being nonsensical. The deed had obviously been done under cover of night. She bent down and righted the small casket that had contained her jewels, now distressingly empty.

Her shock slowly faded, with anger taking its place. "The wretched villain," she cried, "sneaking in here while I slept but yards away." The mere idea of such a thing caused a shiver to work its way up her spine.

She turned to glare at Spotted Bert. "And you, Bertie! A fine watchdog you are! It would not surprise me if you had licked the villain's hands and then helped retrieve things to put into his sack."

Bertie cocked his head, appearing to be confused by the reproachful tone.

"You might at least have barked. Goodness knows, you are never quiet on any other occasion."

Gwenda broke off her scolding as a thought struck her. Mayhap Bertie had barked and she had been so deeply asleep she hadn't heard him. But what about Colette? Surely she must have noticed something was amiss.

Gwenda's eyes traveled toward her maid's cot and she stiffened. So startled had she been upon first entering the room to find her trunks rifled, she had not noticed the smooth linen sheets turned carefully back, the feather-tick pillow plumped to perfection. It was obvious Colette's bed had not even been slept in last night.

As Gwenda stared at the cot, unwelcome suspicions began to sift into her mind. The untouched bed, the odd-tasting glass of milk Colette had pressed upon her, her heavy sleep that was almost as though she had swallowed a good dose of laudanum or some other drug.

Feeling much troubled, Gwenda sank back on her heels and wrapped her arms about her dog's neck. "No, it won't do, Bertie, to go leaping to conclusions without proof. I know it looks bad that Colette is not here, but then she never is when I want her. Why, for all I know the poor girl could have been kidnapped by the thieves. As Mama would say, a good general would never court-martial anyone without first obtaining all the facts."

Gwenda rose thoughtfully to her feet and walked back to her own room. At least her wrapper was still there, laid out over the back of the chair. She tugged the soft peach-colored robe over her linen nightgown and looked for her slippers, but they were gone.

"I do trust that was the thief at work," she said sternly to her dog, "and not you, Bertie."

Spotted Bert allowed his tongue to loll out, assuming his most innocent expression.

Gwenda strode past the dog. Opening her door, she stepped into the corridor and was fortunate enough to encounter one of the inn's chambermaids, a strapping country lass with blooming cheeks and a cheery smile. She bustled past with an armload of fresh towels. Gwenda, who had a knack for recalling names, even down to the lowest menial in the kitchens, remembered that the girl's name was Sallie.

She summoned the girl to her side and asked, "Sallie, have you seen my maid belowstairs this morning?"

"Mamzelle Colette? No, miss. I'm sure I haven't." The girl sniffed. There was a disdainful edge in her voice that Gwenda had oft heard from other female servants when they spoke of Colette.

"Oh, dear," Gwenda said. "Well, I'm afraid something dreadful has happened." She beckoned for the girl to follow her into Colette's room, where she exhibited her empty trunks.

"You will perceive," she said calmly, "that I have been robbed."

Gwenda was completely unprepared for the maid's spectacular reaction. Sallie emitted a small shriek and dropped her towels. Turning pale with horror, she shrank back against the wall, clasping her hands over her bosom.

"Oh, lawks, miss. Lawks!"

"You needn't act as though I've just shown you a dead body," Gwenda said, growing a trifle impatient with these Cheltenham theatrics. "Though I will admit the thought of a sneak thief is most distressing. And the disappearance of my maid only further complicates the matter."

"Oh, miss!" Sallie exclaimed again.

"And I am not quite sure how I ought to proceed," Gwenda said, thoughts of constables and

Bow Street Runners chasing around in her brain. In any event, she saw that the excitable chambermaid was not going to be of much help beyond wringing her large hands and moaning "Oh, miss! Oh, miss!" at suitable intervals.

Gwenda supposed she could begin by determining exactly what had been taken. As she squatted down, she thought ruefully that that was not going to be difficult since, in truth, not much of her belongings had been left. The jewels and money, of course, were gone and most of her clothes except for her second-best bonnet and a drab merino traveling gown. She could not help reflecting on how Colette had always regarded those particular articles of her clothing with scorn.

Aside from that, she found the copies of her novels scattered by the bed, her chipped ivory hairbrush, and a pair of stockings with a hole in it. But just beneath the stockings she saw the glint of an object that made her cry out with joy.

Her pearl-handled pistol! The thief had somehow missed or discarded it. It had been a special gift from her mother.

"A general's granddaughter ought to know how to use a weapon, Gwenda," Mama had said. "Those books you write are quite entertaining, all about how the dashing hero rescues the fair lady at the last possible moment. But the sad truth is, my love, that a gentleman can never be depended upon to arrive for anything on time."

Dearest Mama. Always so practical, Gwenda thought as she scooped up the pistol. Somehow the loss of everything else did not quite matter so much now. She raised the pistol in her hands, cocking back the hammer, and lovingly tested the balance of the finely wrought weapon.

She momentarily forgot the presence of the jittery chambermaid, nor did it occur to her that she was leveling the muzzle directly at Sallie until the girl let loose an ear-splitting scream.

Only minutes earlier, several doors down, the newly arisen Ravenel, garbed in his scarlet brocade dressing gown, had lathered his face with shaving soap. Bending toward a small cheval glass, he cautiously wielded a straight-edged razor beneath his chin.

It had been some time since Jarvis's hands were steady enough to perform this task for his master. It stretched the baron's ingenuity considerably to find excuses why he should shave himself, inventing other pressing duties for Jarvis that would salvage the old man's pride.

This morning Ravenel had been unable to think of anything else better than expressing an earnest desire that Jarvis read aloud to him. Regrettably, the only material available for such an exercise seemed to be Miss Vickers's wretched book. Jarvis appeared momentarily astonished by the request, but then he obeyed with alacrity, intoning Miss Vickers's nonsense as though he were reading a sermon from the pulpit.

" '. . . and the dismembered hand crept nearer and nearer to the terrified maiden, a trail of blood dripping from its severed stump—' "

"Good Lord!" Ravenel muttered. What a ghoulish imagination Miss Vickers had. He wasn't certain he cared to hear about blood and dismemberment when he was wielding a razor so close to his own throat. "Er, Jarvis, skip that bit. Go further ahead."

"Very good, my lord."

Was it Ravenel's imagination or did his valet sound disappointed? As his lordship negotiated the sharp steel over the curve of his jaw, he heard the rustling of pages.

"This part in Volume Two must be of exceptional quality, my lord," Jarvis said. "I see that Miss Vickers has taken some pains to mark it."

The baron opened his lips to protest, but Jarvis had already begun to read. " 'Count Delvadoro drew the fair Emeraude against his manly bosom. The soft glow of adoration in his handsome blue eyes made the lady long to weep for joy.' "

Ravenel pursed his lips. That Vickers woman was always going on about eyes, he thought, remembering her comment about his own. He couldn't refrain from stealing a furtive glance into the mirror, studying the skeptical dark depths reflected back at him. Did she really think that his eyes were . . .

Ravenel drew back feeling sheepish and disgusted with himself.

" 'The count pressed his lips fervently against Emeraude's fingertips,' " Jarvis read in bland tones. " ' "Oh, my heart's treasure," said he. "If you will not consent to be my own, I shall—" ' "

The count's intentions were lost in the next instant, interrupted by the sound of a woman's

63

muffled scream. Ravenel was so startled that he very nearly sliced off his nose.

"What the devil!" He swore and grabbed a handkerchief to stem the drops of blood where he had nicked himself. His eyes met Jarvis's alarmed gaze.

"I don't know, my lord." The valet rolled his eyes to the book in his lap as though he half feared the sound had emanated from the pages of *The Dark Hand* itself.

Ravenel heard a flurry of movement in the corridor beyond. As he strode toward his door, he could not begin to guess what the commotion was, but he harbored a dreadful certainty that he was going to find Gwenda Mary Vickers the source of it.

He flung open the door and stepped into the hall, only to be nearly knocked down by a fleeing chambermaid gibbering like a terrified monkey.

"Come back here at once, you goose," a familiar feminine voice shouted at the maid.

Miss Vickers erupted from her room, brandishing a pistol.

Good God, Ravenel thought as the chambermaid dove behind him with a frightened squeak. That Vickers woman was more crazed than he had feared.

As she waved the pistol at his chest, Ravenel sucked in his breath, bracing himself for a loud report and the feel of a ball searing though his flesh.

Miss Vickers's eyes flashed scornfully as she peered past him at the cowering chambermaid. " 'Tis not loaded, you idiotic girl." Her assurance did nothing to calm the maid, who went off into hysterics, but the baron sighed with relief.

All the same, he caught Gwenda's wrist and carefully forced her to lower the weapon to her side. "What the deuce are you doing with a thing like that?" he growled.

"My mother gave it to me," Miss Vickers said, as though that explained everything. "It was a present for my last birthday."

Ravenel swallowed an urge to point out to her that most mothers gave their daughters gifts like pearls or parasols. "No. I meant, why are you—"

But his question was broken off since by this time the other guests staying at the Hart came rushing out into the hallway: a stout dowager clutching her wrapper about her, her scrawny daughter hard on her heels; several elderly gentlemen still wearing their nightcaps; and from Ravenel's own room, Jarvis, adjusting his spectacles to peer with interest at Miss Vickers. Everyone spoke at once, demanding to know what had happened in varying tones of fear and indignation. To add to the din, the chambermaid continued to wail and Miss Vickers's dog leaped about, setting up a fearful barking.

Mr. Leatherbury charged onto the scene, his round face flushed red from the unaccustomed exertion of running up the stairs.

"What?" he said, huffing. "What is the meaning of all this?" His gaze traveled from the pistol still gripped in Gwenda's hand to Ravenel's face. The baron became conscious of a fresh trickle of blood going down his chin and groped for his handkerchief again.

"Miss Vickers!" the landlord said in shocked accents. "Never tell me you have gone and shot at his lordship."

"Don't be preposterous," Ravenel muttered from behind his handkerchief.

"Certainly not," Miss Vickers said. " 'Tis just that I have been robbed."

Her blunt statement caused a fresh sensation: more outcries from the other guests, more sobs from the chambermaid, and more barking from Bertie.

"Robbed?" Leatherbury said, his face turning purple with outrage. "Here at the White Hart? Impossible, Miss Vickers. Quite impossible."

"It is very possible, you silly man," Gwenda retorted. "You have but to go look in my room."

In the face of Leatherbury's obvious disbelief, even the imperturbable Miss Vickers began to get a trifle agitated. A most spirited quarrel developed between her and the host of the White Hart. Several of the waiters and the boots came crowding into the corridor to add their voices to the hubbub.

"Eh? What's happened here?"

"Dunno . . . think one of the guests has been robbed."

"Brigands!" the dowager shrieked. "We might all have been murdered in our beds."

"Nonsense. Utter nonsense," Leatherbury replied huffily.

Ravenel had had all that he was prepared to endure. He was not accustomed to tolerating confusion, especially not in the morning before he had even had his coffee and beefsteak.

"Quiet!" he thundered.

The authoritative tone of his command immediately reduced everyone to silence. Even Bertie subsided after one more small yap. Ravenel took advantage of the hush to snap out a series of brisk orders that sent the waiters back to their posts and the other guests scurrying for their rooms. He had the boots lead away the sniveling chambermaid and put Jarvis in charge of Bertie. Strangely enough, even the dog seemed to recognize the dignity of Jarvis, for Bertie went quietly without offering to leap upon him.

Then the baron strode back to Gwenda and Leatherbury. All traces of her annoyance with the landlord had faded, and she greeted Ravenel, her eyes glowing.

"Well done!" she said, clapping her hands with enthusiasm. "You're so awfully good at that."

"Good at what?" he asked, taken aback.

"Ordering people about, taking charge. You were just like some magnificent Turkish despot in your scarlet brocade. You looked most formidable rapping out commands even if there is still a small bit of shaving soap clinging to your chin."

Ravenel wondered if she was mocking him, but there was no doubting the sincerity of her admiration or the warmth of her smile. He flushed, his fingers moving self-consciously from the lapel of his dressing gown up to wipe at his chin. Damn the woman. She had a positive talent for disconcerting him.

He chose to ignore her comments, saying gruffly, "Now, Miss Vickers. What is all this nonsense about being robbed?"

" 'Tisn't nonsense. Follow me and I'll show you." Gesturing with her pistol, Miss Vickers led the way back to her room. The baron followed her, with Leatherbury hard after him, still mumbling, "Ridiculous. Impossible. Not at my inn."

But the landlord's manner changed rapidly when they stood looking down at the overturned trunks in the maid's room. He blanched and stammered, "B-but . . . I can scarcely credit my eyes. I—I . . . my dear, dear Miss Vickers. Do forgive me. That such a thing should have happened to you *here* at the White Hart."

Leatherbury proceeded to ply her with everything from a glass of wine to sal volatile. But the landlord looked in far greater need of smelling salts than Miss Vickers did. Ravenel could not help noticing that even under these trying circumstances Miss Vickers had a most becoming tint of rose in her cheeks. She waved aside all of the landlord's solicitude.

"You needn't worry, Mr. Leatherbury. I have never swooned in my life—not even the time my brother shot me in the foot with an arrow."

Ravenel, who had begun to make a cursory examination of one of the trunks, paused. He knew he would be better off not inquiring further into this startling statement, but his curiosity got the better of him.

"Your brother shot you with an arrow?" he repeated.

"It was over a wager. Jack thought that if I

68

held a quill pen between my toes, he could nick off the top of the feathers." She sighed. "Of course, that was a long time ago, but I've never since had quite the same confidence in Jack."

"I—I daresay," Mr. Leatherbury said faintly.

Miss Vickers brightened. "But my father has bought Jack a commission in the army. I hope he will learn to have better aim with a musket."

Heaven help the British army, Ravenel thought, turning his attention back to the matter at hand. The maid's bed was obviously unslept in, the trunks opened by someone who had access to the keys and didn't have to force the locks. The conclusion was obvious to him, but all he said was, "And where is your maid this morning, Miss Vickers?"

"I don't know." She added, almost too quickly, "But that doesn't necessarily prove anything against her."

Ravenel thought it proved a great deal. He said, "I suggest we take steps to find the girl immediately. Leatherbury, you might begin by making inquiries among your servants. And the constable had best be sent for."

"Aye, at once, my lord." The distracted host appeared only too eager to be doing something. He rushed out still lamenting, "A robbery! Here! At my inn."

Miss Vickers sank down upon the cot, ruefully biting her lip. "The poor man. I feel quite guilty somehow for having brought this distress upon him."

"You might have had the consideration to be

robbed elsewhere, Miss Vickers," Ravenel agreed drily. "Most unkind of you."

She regarded him in surprise, then her ready smile flashed up at him. "Why, Lord Ravenel. You do possess a sense of humor after all."

His lips twitched in response to the marveling tone of her voice. It occurred to him that Miss Vickers looked rather charming for a lady who had just tumbled out of bed. Her chestnut curls danced about her flushed cheeks in appealing disarray, nigh tempting a man to smooth back the silken tangles from her brow. The peach-colored wrapper but served to highlight the creaminess of her skin along her delicate collarbone and graceful neckline. And as for the way the soft lawn night shift clung to the full curve of her breast . . .

Ravenel averted his gaze, embarrassed by the direction his thoughts were taking, and suddenly aware of the impropriety of their situation: alone in the maid's room, neither of them decently garbed.

The baron tugged at the sash binding his brocade dressing gown and cleared his throat. "Ahem. Well, you'd best summon that witling chambermaid to help you dress. You do have something left to wear, don't you?"

"Yes." Gwenda plucked a drab-looking gown from the floor, regarding it with little enthusiasm.

"Then I will meet you belowstairs and we can decide how best to proceed."

Her dark lashes swept up as she shot him a look of mingled astonishment and gratitude.

"Thank you, Lord Ravenel. 'Tis most gallant of you to concern yourself in this matter."

"Not in the least," he muttered, and then exited somewhat awkwardly from the room. If Gwenda was surprised by his behavior, Ravenel was astounded. What was he doing meddling in this business when his only desire was to avoid the eccentric Miss Vickers? He put his interference down to an irrational feeling of guilt. He could not help remembering that look he had seen on the maid's face the night before, the impulse to warn Miss Vickers that he had suppressed.

Not that he intended to be drawn too far into this affair. No, he would simply see to it that some responsible person was put in charge of helping the lady and then he would be on his way to Brighton.

After returning to his own room, he explained briefly what had happened as Jarvis helped him to dress. The old man clucked his tongue sympathetically. "Poor Miss Vickers."

"Yes," Ravenel agreed with an absent frown, noticing for the first time that Bertie was still in his room. The dog had made himself quite comfortable, falling asleep on the baron's bed. Bertie didn't stir until Ravenel made ready to leave. Then the dog stood up, yawned, and followed him.

Anyone would think the beast belonged to *him*, Ravenel thought, grimacing, as he made his way downstairs. He found Miss Vickers already there, ensconced in the same private parlor that had witnessed their first unfortuitous encounter the day before.

Garbed in that unbecoming maroon gown, she sat in a straight-backed chair fingering her bonnet with a most forlorn expression on her face. She scarcely took notice of the cup of tea the solicitous Leatherbury placed upon the table beside her.

When Ravenel entered, the host met his questioning look with a frown. "The maid seems to have vanished, my lord, and Miss Vickers has been telling me her fears that a sleep-inducing agent was introduced into her milk last night. We have no choice but to conclude that Mademoiselle Colette was the culprit."

This information occasioned the baron no surprise, but Miss Vickers's expression did. Earlier she had not been in the least perturbed to find her belongings plundered; now she appeared excessively troubled.

She fetched a heavy sigh. " 'Tis not that I mind so much about my things—'twas only a parcel of frocks and fripperies after all. But it is most distressing to be hoodwinked by a person one knew and trusted."

Aye, thought Ravenel. Miss Vickers, for all her grim imaginings about villains and evildoers, was exactly the sort of lady who would trust everyone, who cherished complete faith in her fellow creatures. As he observed the puzzled hurt welling in her luminous green eyes, he was astonished to feel a strong urge to find that ungrateful French trollop and wring her neck.

He strode up to Gwenda, took her hand, and

patted it. "My dear Miss Vickers, a dishonest wench like that is hardly worth fretting over. I am sure it will be only a matter of time before she receives her just punishment and your belongings are returned."

Gwenda glanced up at Ravenel, astonished by both the gesture and the gentleness of his tone. The kindness and sympathy on his face did much to mitigate the natural severity of his features. She wondered if the man had any notion how devastating his eyes were when they glowed softly like that. His hand was quite large and strong, engulfing her slender fingers in a warm clasp. She felt oddly breathless and had difficulty concentrating on what he was saying.

"Mayhap there might be some clue in your maid's background, Miss Vickers. Who referred her to your service?"

His palms were slightly callused, very likely from riding. She could picture him masterfully gathering up the reins of a fiery black stallion, its glossy mane the same midnight color as his hair.

"Miss Vickers?" Ravenel prodded gently.

Gwenda came out of her daydreaming with a start. He had been asking her something. What was it? Oh, yes. Colette's character reference.

"She didn't have one."

"Didn't have one!" the baron echoed, looking nonplussed.

"No, we met her one day in a millinery shop. Mama hired her because she spoke such beautiful French."

Neither Ravenel nor Mr. Leatherbury appeared to be following her logic, so Gwenda explained patiently, "My mother is deeply concerned about Napoleon, the threat of a French invasion. She thought it would be good if we perfected our command of the language."

"But—but," Mr. Leatherbury protested, "why didn't she engage a tutor?"

"I didn't need a tutor," Gwenda said. "I needed a maid."

Ravenel's mouth snapped shut. He dropped her hand as though she had suddenly contracted some contagious disease.

"Of all the cork-brained—" He drew himself up erect and fixed her with a stern eye. "Are you giving me to understand that you simply plucked this woman out of the streets?"

"Not out of the streets," Gwenda said, resenting his tone. "Out of a hat shop."

He shook his head in disgust. "Then I fear you have gotten exactly what you deserved, Miss Vickers."

Gwenda was stunned by his change of attitude. But if he had suddenly lost all sympathy for her, she was beginning to feel quite out of charity with him, especially when he launched into a long homily about the folly of hiring servants without references.

This was Lord Ravenel at his positively most stuffy, Gwenda thought. When he squared his shoulders in that pompous manner, she longed to stick a pin into him. She crossed her arms over her chest, wondering how such a man could ever have made her heart skip a beat, even for the barest instant.

The baron was so caught up in lecturing her that he appeared not to notice the ostler who slipped into the room and beckoned to Mr. Leatherbury. Whatever the burly groom whispered to the landlord, poor Leatherbury went chalk-white, darting a glance of terror at his lordship.

". . . and I have never had a servant in my employ," Ravenel was saying, "upon whose character I could not stake my own reputation."

"M-my lord," Leatherbury said. He approached the baron with all the abject timidity of a rabbit coming to impart bad tidings to a fierce-maned lion. When the host momentarily lost his power of speech, Ravenel prompted impatiently, "Yes, man. What is it?"

"M-more misfortune, your lordship." Leatherbury swallowed. "W-we now know how the wench made her escape. S-she t-took your phaeton and . . . ," the host concluded in a voice that was barely audible, "your bays."

"My bays?" Ravenel choked, then repeated in a much louder voice, "*My bays!* Your grooms allowed that scheming baggage to take my horses!"

Leatherbury cowered away from him. Even Gwenda felt herself tense at the fury vibrating in the baron's voice. So that was how a man looked when he is enraged enough to commit murder with his bare hands. She had gotten that all wrong in her second book.

The ostler spoke up. "Nay, me lud. 'Twas one o' the young stable lads wot made the mistake. 'Twas during the confusion when the night stage was coming through. The girl had yer ludship's tiger with her, a-wearing yer own livery and he

75

says as how they was off to fetch a doctor fer yer ludship."

"My tiger?" Ravenel repeated numbly. "Dalton?"

"Aye, the same, me lud."

Gwenda tried to remain nobly silent but couldn't. "How shocking! I suppose the man had a great many character references, Lord Ravenel?" she inquired sweetly.

His lordship spun around, the fierceness of his gaze causing Gwenda to shrink back in her chair. "It so happens I dismissed that man from my service just yesterday, Miss Vickers. But as to character, Dalton was quite satisfactory until your doxy of a maid got her hooks into him."

"I suppose Colette abducted your Dalton and forced him to steal your horses and . . ." Gwenda paused in the midst of her indignant little speech, and mulled it over in her mind. "Goodness, that would be a diverting twist to a tale, wouldn't it? I wonder what my publisher would think."

She wasn't sure, but she could tell full well what Ravenel thought. His mouth was pinched together in a thin white line to keep from cursing aloud.

"Where the dev— Where is that constable, Leatherbury?"

"I-I'll just find out what's keeping him, my lord." Leatherbury scuttled out with Ravenel hard upon his heels. Gwenda bit back a smile. She liked the baron much better when he was on a rampage than when one of his stuffy spells came over him. She supposed it was too bad of

76

her to have teased him. The loss of some small change and clothing was nothing compared to the loss of a fine pair of blooded horses.

But she doubted a village constable was going to prove of much help to his lordship. He would be better off pursuing the miscreants himself or hiring a professional thief-taker.

The only bright spot of the morning came when her footman James sought her out to tell her the carriage brace had been fixed. She could depart for Brighton any time she was ready, which was not likely to be long, Gwenda thought philosophically. It was not as though she had a great deal to pack.

With Bertie whisking by her side, Gwenda was on her way upstairs to do so, when the boots passed by her, going down. The lanky young man appeared just as agitated as the rest of the inn staff by all the untoward happenings.

"Ain't it just awful, miss?" the boots moaned. "Such doings at the White Hart I never thought to see. And to top it all, someone's gone and pinched one of them Hessians his lordship gave me to polish. I ask you, what would anyone want with just one boot?"

Thankfully, the man rushed on his way without waiting for an answer, as Gwenda felt a flush steal into her cheeks. She froze upon the stair, glancing down at her dog. "Oh, Bertie," she whispered. "You didn't."

The innocent wag of his tail told her nothing, but she knew Bertie could contrive to look unconcerned even with bits of leather sticking between his teeth. With a sinking feeling she returned to her own room.

She finally located Ravenel's boot under the bed she had slept in. The rolled-down leather top looked as though it had been attacked by a party of rabid squirrels.

"Bertie, how could you?" Gwenda moaned. "Out of all the guests at this inn, why did you have to single out Lord Ravenel's boot?"

Bertie whined and hung his head, looking suitably ashamed.

"I've seen that performance before," she said bitterly. "Half the actors at Drury Lane should do remorse so well. No, get away. I will not pet you, sir. You have sunk yourself completely beneath reproach this time."

She snatched up the boot and thrust the dog out of her path. Bertie trailed after her as she marched into the hall, squaring her shoulders. Well, mayhap if she was lucky, she would find Jarvis first. She had a feeling the elderly valet would accept the return of the Hessian much more kindly than Ravenel would.

But her luck was out. There was no sign of the dignified valet. The baron was far more easy to locate. Gwenda discovered him in the stableyard, shouting at the unfortunate Leatherbury.

"What do you mean there are no post-horses available?"

The landlord's cherubic face quivered. He appeared about to burst into tears. "I am sorry, my lord, but there isn't a one. I don't even have a horse of my own to lend you. The best I could do is a farmer's donkey or . . . or if you would care to wait, something might be had from the next village."

"I don't care to wait. Between your ostler's carelessness and that fool of a constable, I have been delayed here long enough."

Gwenda crept up behind Ravenel, holding the boot behind her back. Now she understood how poor Mr. Leatherbury must have felt earlier when he had to tell his lordship about his stolen bays.

"Lord Ravenel!" she called.

He stiffened at the sound of her voice. Then he spun about and favored her with an impatient glance. "What is it, Miss Vickers?"

"I—I found your other boot."

"I wasn't aware the blasted thing was missing."

She nodded unhappily and fetched the Hessian from behind her back.

"Thank you," he said curtly, taking the boot and starting to tuck it under his arm. He paused, his eyes arrested by the teeth marks on the top. Then his gaze shifted from the ravaged leather to where Bertie stood beside her panting, his tongue hanging in a foolish dog's grin.

Ravenel clenched his jaw until it quivered. Something seemed to explode inside of him.

"Damnation!" he bellowed.

So the man could swear after all, Gwenda thought, taking an awed step backward. "I—I am so sorry."

"Sorry!" His lordship strode a little away from her, his hands tightening on the boot as he strove to compose himself.

"Please. I know you've had an absolutely beastly time of it and 'tis partly my fault," Gwenda said, following him. "If you would only allow me to make amends. I could not help overhearing Mr. Leatherbury just now about the posthorses. My carriage is repaired. I could take you—"

"Certainly not," Ravenel ground out between his teeth. "I desire nothing except that you should keep your distance from me, madam. You—you are the absolute mistress of disaster!"

Gwenda flinched as if he had struck her. Before he said anything more that he would regret, Ravenel stalked back inside the inn, where Jarvis awaited him in the private parlor.

The baron plunked the damaged boot down. "Get rid of this thing."

Jarvis said nothing but quietly disposed of the Hessian. "I have ordered your lordship's breakfast."

"I am not in the least hungry," Ravenel snapped. Indeed, he had a strong suspicion that even the most delectable beefsteak would have tasted like old shoe leather at that particular moment. He knew he was behaving like a temperamental schoolboy, and that realization did naught to soften his mood.

Not that he truly cared a damn about what that blasted hound had done to his boot. It was just the final blow to an already foul morning. Not only was his journey delayed another day, but he had lost his bays. He had been quite proud of those horses. Perfectly matched, they had cost him a tidy sum.

But he wasn't even sure if it was their theft that gnawed at him as much as knowing what a prize fool he had been made to look. Lecturing Miss Vickers about her servant and then to have one of his own commit a far greater crime . . .

Jarvis's gentle voice broke into his disquieting reflections. "You had no luck then, my lord, in obtaining another conveyance?"

"None, unless you wish to jog along by common stage or in a cart behind a farmer's donkey."

"I should not mind it, my lord," Jarvis said valiantly.

"But I should."

No, as much as Ravenel loathed the prospect of lingering about the White Hart, he knew he could not expose his valet to the hardships of the stage or the donkey. "Of course, we could always take Miss Vickers up on her generous offer," he said sarcastically.

"What was that, my lord?"

"To travel with her in her carriage."

To Ravenel's extreme consternation, Jarvis looked pleased by the suggestion. "That would be most kind of your lordship," the valet said. "I owned I have been concerned about that unfortunate young lady. Losing all her money and now no maid in attendance, left to travel all on her own."

"You might as well be concerned about Boadicea, the warrior queen." Ravenel snorted. "I'll wager she left far less havoc in her wake."

"The young lady does seem to have a penchant for getting into trouble, my lord. All the more reason she should not be permitted to journey to Brighton alone."

"That is her family's responsibility—not mine."

"Very good, my lord," Jarvis said. There was a shade of disapproval in his valet's eyes that Ravenel had never seen there before.

He squirmed, made most uncomfortable by it. Blast it, Jarvis didn't even know the half of it. Ravenel had never sworn or behaved with incivility to any female before. Miss Vickers had induced him to do both within twenty-four hours of her acquaintance.

Disquieting memories of the recent scene in the inn yard flashed through his mind. Gwenda meekly offering him the boot, trying desperately to apologize; the look of hurt in her eyes when he had lashed out at her. He would have to beg her pardon for that, but as to traveling with her ... No, if for no other reason, it would be dashed improper.

He had an impulse simply to pen her a note of apology. It would be so much safer than going near the woman again, but his conscience would not allow for any such shirking.

At first he hoped—nay, *feared*, he amended—that she had already gone. But he encountered her coming down the inn stairs, swinging what was obviously an empty bandbox. She was wearing a bonnet that was nigh as hideous as her dress. The huge poke seemed to swallow her head, making the piquant face sheltered beneath it seem absurdly youthful, like a little girl got up in her mother's things. Her usually candid green eyes regarded him with a wariness that made him feel even more of a perfect brute.

He approached her stiffly. "Miss Vickers, I want to apologize for my behavior in the inn yard just now."

She gave him an uncertain half smile. "Oh, no. You had every right to be angry. It was terrible of Bertie, and I would be only too happy to pay—"

"I had no right," he said firmly. "you have suffered as much by these recent events as I have, and much more graciously, I might add. Please say that you forgive me."

"Of course I do." She held out her hand, her smile broadening into her customary expression of good humor. Ravenel thought it was rather like watching the sun breaking through the clouds on a dismal day and was astonished at the poetical turn his mind seemed to have taken of late.

Instead of merely shaking her hand, he carried it to his lips and brushed her long, slender fingertips with a kiss, thus surprising himself again. It was a gallant gesture he rarely felt comfortable according any lady.

Miss Vickers neither blushed not simpered in the annoying way of most society misses. Her green eyes sparkled with pleasure.

She gave his hand a squeeze. "Good. I am so glad we are friends again. Now mayhap you will reconsider my offer to make use of my carriage."

" 'Tis very kind of you, but it would not be proper," he explained patiently as though to a child. "You see, you have no female companion with you."

"But we would be in Brighton before nightfall. And if anyone asked"—Gwenda nodded toward a point beyond his shoulder—"we could tell them that your Jarvis there is my uncle. Such a distinguished-looking man. I should not mind at all claiming him for my relative."

Ravenel glanced around to see that Jarvis had come up behind him. The elderly manservant was blushing like a peony.

Ravenel shook his head. "No. I fear, Miss Vickers, such proceedings would be most unwise."

"Oh, please. At least let me convey you to another inn where you could hire a post chaise. I do feel so wretchedly responsible for the fix you are in."

The baron prided himself on being rigid to the point of inflexibility once he had made a decision. But he had never in his life encountered such wide, pleading green-gold eyes. Well, he thought, relenting, what harm could it do to go at least part of the way with Miss Vickers and make sure she was headed safely on the way to her destination this time.

"Very well." He sighed. "If you do not mind waiting a few moments while I gather up my things."

Jarvis looked pleased, Miss Vickers delighted. The only one yet suffering from qualms was Ravenel himself. But what could possibly happen between here and the next town?

He clung to that sanguine opinion until he saw Miss Vickers's equipage being brought around. It was a spanking new coach, and smart enough. But the footman who tossed the baron's portmanteau up onto the back was a scruffy, ill-favored lad, half drowning in a livery too large for him, the sleeve of which showed signs of being employed as a handkerchief.

Yet it was the coachman, Fitch, who was Ravenel's chief concern. The man perched upon his box. Beside him Spotted Bert panted as though eager for the journey to begin. The dog looked far more ready than Fitch. The poker-stiff coachman's tensed hands knotted about the reins in a way that Ravenel knew marked the most amateur of whips.

As for the team, his lordship's expert eyes knew a mismatched set when he saw it. He would have wagered his last groat that those restive wheelers were beset with a tendency to break into a gallop every chance they got.

This is a grave mistake, a stern voice warned him, but Miss Vickers was smiling up at him, waiting to be handed into the coach. Ravenel had no choice but to do so, then spring up after her, as he wondered what he had let himself in for now.

# Chapter 4

As the carriage lumbered away from God-stone, Gwenda settled back against the squabs, wondering why she felt so absurdly pleased with herself. Mayhap it was a sense of satisfaction from having persuaded one of the stubbornest men in England to change his mind; mayhap it simply soothed her conscience to be able to make some amends to his lordship after all the difficulties she had brought down upon him: the eavesdropping, the stolen bays, the ravaged boot.

But it was a satisfaction his lordship obviously did not share. Tensed into an attitude of pained resignation, Ravenel sat opposite her, his broad shoulders braced against the gentle sway of the well-sprung carriage. The reed-thin Jarvis appeared quite lost in his master's shadow, as Ravenel's large frame seemed to dominate the coach. Gwenda was conscious of her knees almost brushing against his, of the tight-fitting doeskin trousers that emphasized the muscular outline of his legs.

Gwenda was obliged to admit the real reason

she took pleasure in Ravenel's accompanying her. The man intrigued her, with his stiff mannerisms so at odds with his gypsy-dark eyes, the humor and the temper that he took such pains to suppress even if it well nigh choked him, the gruffness that concealed a shyness, an uncertainty she found rather endearing in such a formidable-looking gentleman. Before they arrived at their destination, Gwenda resolved to coax him into relaxing the rigidity that threatened to carve premature age lines about his mouth and eyes and to wring at least one smile from the man.

As though becoming aware of her earnest regard, Ravenel shifted uncomfortably on his seat and then stared out the window with frowning concentration. His long fingers drummed upon his knee, beating out an impatient rhythm.

"Miss Vickers, I don't wish to sound as though I'm complaining," he said, "but if we continue along at such a snail's pace, I doubt any of us will reach Brighton this side of Michaelmas."

"Certainly we will. We always travel this slowly and still arrive well before nightfall. You see, Fitch—" Gwenda broke off and coughed discreetly into her hand. She had been in Ravenel's company long enough to realize he might find it unsettling to be told that her coachman was afraid of horses. She continued, "Fitch is a most cautious driver because my dog oft gets down to run with the carriage. Our nearest neighbor, Squire Bennington, tried to train Bertie as a coaching dog, but I am afraid he found Bertie rather lacking in—in *gentlemanly reserve*, so he gave the dog to me."

A chuckle escaped Gwenda. "Sometimes Bertie even—" She halted again. She'd best not mention that, either—that instead of running beneath the rear axle, her reckless dog would insinuate himself under the pole tip and race the forefeet of the wheelers and the leaders' flying hooves, wreaking such havoc on poor Fitch's nerves that he needed a drop of whiskey to steady himself. No, that bit of information would not help Ravenel to relax. His lordship already had little cause to be fond of Bertie.

But she had paused so long in her answer, she found the baron regarding her rather suspiciously. She swallowed and then concluded brightly, "Ah, sometimes Bertie runs the longest distances. You would be quite astounded."

"I sincerely trust not, Miss Vickers," Ravenel said with some feeling. "I have been astounded enough for one day."

"Of course," she said demurely, folding her hands in her lap and reassuring herself how right she was to withhold certain facts from his lordship. After all, Fitch had faithfully promised after the last time that he would never get foxed again.

The next instant the coach veered sharply to the left. Gwenda bumped her shoulder against the side and straightened, rubbing her bruised arm. She was well accustomed to the peculiarities of Fitch's driving.

Ravenel, however, appeared a little alarmed as he eased back Jarvis, who had thumped against him. His lordship peered out the window again, exclaiming, "What the deuce is your coachman doing, Miss Vickers? Why has he taken this turning off the main road?" Ravenel started to thump on the roof to get Fitch's attention, but Gwenda caught his sleeve.

"No, 'tis quite all right, Lord Ravenel. We always travel by the old route through East Grinstead, Uckfield, and Lewes."

"That's the longer way," he protested.

"Aye, but the road is in excellent condition and there is much less traffic."

And much less chance that Fitch would get them lost if they stuck to the old route. But Gwenda buried that thought behind an ingenuous smile. "Don't worry so, Lord Ravenel. I promise you we shall all be making merry in Brighton before the sun sets. I am sure you can hire yourself a rig as easily in East Grinstead as anywhere else."

"I suppose so." The baron settled back uneasily. "But I would think that Lord and Lady Vickers—at least *most* parents—would be concerned about their daughter after such an unexpected delay. I cannot think what they are about, letting you travel alone."

There it was again—that certain sharp edge, that hint of criticism that came into Ravenel's voice whenever he mentioned anything about her family.

"I am not alone." Gwenda bridled. "I have Fitch and James and Bertie, and I did have Colette. 'Twas only to have been a simple day's journey from my aunt's home in Richmond."

She winced at the memory. "I am fond of my Aunt Lucinda, but a more dreary house party you could not have imagined. There was a young man present who was about to write a book. I always seem to be introduced to someone who is just about to write a book. Mr. Pomfret spent hours regaling me with the plot—" Gwenda halted as a horrible fear struck her.

"You do not, by any chance, write, do you, Lord Ravenel? "

Ravenel's mouth twitched. "No, Miss Vickers. Naught but business letters."

"Thank goodness," she breathed. "Now if Jarvis does not, either, I shall feel quite safe."

The valet assured her most gravely that he was not that clever. For the first time, she noticed that among his lordship's belongings—his whip, riding gloves, and hat—that Jarvis had taken personal charge of, the first volume of her novel was included.

Gwenda glanced at Ravenel. "Oh! So you have been reading the book I gave you?"

The was a long pause and then he said, "I scarcely have had time to look at it. Quite frankly, Miss Vickers, I am not much interested in fiction, but Jarvis has been finding it most entertain—"

"Why, my lord," Jarvis interrupted. "Begging your pardon, sir, but you had me read you some of it only this morning."

Gwenda beamed at Ravenel in triumph. He shot his valet a quelling frown, but unperturbed, Jarvis continued, "Your lordship did not much care for the part where the hand was running amok, but you appeared to enjoy the scene where the count offered for Lady Emeraude."

"The marriage proposal?" Gwenda exclaimed with delight. "I knew your lordship would find that bit fascinating. Of course, it is somewhat exaggerated for the purposes of fiction, but it does give you some idea how you ought to go on with Miss Carruthers the next time—"

"Miss Vickers!" Ravenel's face suffused a dull red. If he had been relaxed at all, he was immediately all stiffness again. "If you do not mind, I have no desire to discuss my personal affairs."

Gwenda's gaze shifted from his lordship's crimson-stained cheeks to the valet, who was also looking slightly discomfited. "Oh, I see. I am sorry for having mentioned it. I naturally assumed Jarvis knew. My brother Jack confides everything in his valet, and Jarvis certainly looks the sympathetic sort to whom I would tell all my darkest secrets if—"

"Miss Vickers!" The baron let out an exasperated sigh. "Can you not get it through your head? It is you I object to discussing my affairs with. *You!* Besides being practically a stranger, I cannot see where you have had the experience to be offering me advice."

What! Did the man think simply because she was unwed that she had never had an offer? Gwenda drew herself up primly. "Indeed, I have, my lord. It so happens I have been engaged twice."

"Twice!" his lordship and Jarvis both gasped in the same breath. Ravenel's lips parted as though he meant to ask something. Then he appeared to change his mind and feigned a deep interest in the distant farmhouses snuggled into folds of green pastureland.

"Then what—" Jarvis began, then stopped, looking appalled at himself. "I beg your pardon, miss. I never intended to be so forward as to pry. I'm sure there must have been some great tragedy . . ."

"Nothing so dramatic," Gwenda said with a tinkling laugh. "I jilted them."

From the degree of shock that registered on the faces of both men, Gwenda felt she'd best hasten to explain. "I was very young the first time I fancied myself in love, barely sixteen. Jasper was such a delightful companion, but the minute we were engaged, he developed the most distressing habit of sighing and acting like a great cake over me."

"I thought you approved of men who behave so," Ravenel said, rather acidly.

"I like a man to be romantic, not silly. When Jasper took to writing poetry, I simply couldn't bear anymore."

His lordship appeared intrigued in spite of himself. "And the second one? What was his folly?"

"Marlon? His error was even worse." Gwenda offered him a smile brimming with mischief. "The minute the betrothal ring was slipped upon my finger, he started trying to change *me*."

Ravenel regarded her sternly, struggling to keep a straight face. But his mouth quivered, finally breaking into a grin that softened his harsh features. He chuckled. "Miss Vickers! You truly are the most abominable young lady. What shocking bad manners. Ending engagements, leaving a trail of broken hearts . . ."

"But you are laughing," she pointed out.

"So I am," he said, shaking his head at himself. "Much more time in your company and I fear you will have corrupted every notion I have as to what is sane and proper."

"Mayhap you set too high a value upon sanity, my lord."

"Mayhap, I do," Ravenel conceded with another smile.

"And as to broken hearts, both Marlon and Jasper are now quite happily wed. I did them the greatest kindnesses by releasing them." Gwenda became serious suddenly. "There is no greater tragedy than a loveless marriage. I hope that you—" She stopped, for once catching her wayward tongue in time. If she expressed her hope that Ravenel would make sure he was most sincerely in love with Belinda before proposing once more, Gwenda would only set his back up again, which would be a great pity. His lordship looked so devastatingly handsome when he smiled.

Curbing her urge to interfere, Gwenda steered the conversation into safer channels. She soon had both Lord Ravenel and Jarvis chuckling over her trials and tribulations as an authoress. They seemed to find particularly amusing how she had given herself the jitters when writing *The Dark Hand*. It hadn't helped matters the least bit when her brother Jack had suspended a stuffed glove on the end of a broom handle and tapped her on the shoulder with it. He had laid a wager on how far she would jump.

Thus merrily occupied, the time seemed to fly past, and before Gwenda realized it, the carriage had lurched to a halt and James was letting down the steps to help her alight into the stable-yard of the Dorset Arms in East Grinstead.

Ravenel sprung down after her with his elderly valet following at a more sedate pace. Although Jarvis had greatly enjoyed all of Miss Vickers's lively chatter, he had spent the last mile puzzling over the lady's exact relationship to his young master. That his lordship appeared to find Miss Vickers a great nuisance was undoubtedly true, but it had been a long time since Jarvis had seen his master unbend enough to laugh so freely or even to indulge in a fit of temper.

Jarvis judged that Miss Vickers had a way of exploding into a man's life like a burst of fireworks, but he didn't think it would do Master Des any harm to have an occasional skyrocket erupting in his path. For all of Miss Vickers's little oddities, Jarvis quite liked the young lady.

It was with great regret that he watched his master hustle Miss Vickers into the Dorset Arms and settle her into a private parlor before excusing himself to see about the hire of a carriage.

As Ravenel bowed his way across the threshold, Jarvis managed to catch his lordship's eye.

"It does seem such a shame, sir," he whispered, "to be leaving the young lady alone—"

"Don't you start that again," Ravenel hissed. "Miss Vickers will be just fine. 'Tis only another three or four hours to Brighton from here—well, mayhap six the way her coachman drives. But she will arrive by dusk, and I have no intention of dawdling away the rest of my afternoon in this fashion."

Ignoring Jarvis's reproachful look, the baron closed the parlor door and went in quest of the landlord. For the first time since he arose that morning, luck seemed to be with him. The Dorset Arms could indeed provide his lordship with both a curricle and a spanking pair of grays.

Ravenel made arrangements to hire them immediately, steadfastly suppressing all notice of Jarvis's disapproval. By God, that Vickers woman seemed to have done a thorough job of bewitching his valet. Normally a stickler for the proprieties, why couldn't Jarvis see that it simply wouldn't do for the baron to keep trailing about with an unchaperoned lady? It was not as though he were her brother or even a distant cousin.

Besides that, he had all manner of pressing business awaiting him in Brighton, to say nothing of the need to engage some competent person to track down that rascal Dalton before the trail became completely cold. No matter how entertaining Miss Vickers might be—and Ravenel was prepared to concede that at times she was—he simply had no more time to waste.

With such thoughts churning in his head, the baron strode back briskly to the inn parlor to convey his thanks to Miss Vickers for having brought him as far as East Grinstead and to take his final farewell of the lady. He was even feeling gracious enough to express a polite wish that they might meet again one day.

His graciousness vanished when he swung the door open and found the private parlor empty. The luncheon he had ordered for Miss Vickers yet stood upon the oak table untouched.

"Blast the woman!" Ravenel muttered. "Can she never once be doing what is expected of her?"

He swiftly collared one of the waiters only to obtain the vague information that he believed the young lady "was wandering about out in the back somewheres behind the taproom."

Ravenel's mouth pursed into a grim line. Well, it seemed instead of a cordial farewell, he would be obliged to treat Miss Vickers to a lecture on the impropriety of unescorted females roaming too freely at public places.

Exiting through the front door, he quickly directed his footsteps toward the side of the inn opposite the stableyard. Fortunately for his temper, he had no difficulty finding the troublesome female. She was walking through the vegetable garden just outside the kitchen door. Shading her eyes with one hand, she peered at a distant line of birches as though she were looking for something.

The baron squared his jaw and strode purposefully in her direction. But before he had taken many steps, he saw a slim dandy emerge from the taproom. Garbed in a riding cloak with a ridiculous multiplicity of capes, the ginger-haired fop swaggered toward Gwenda, casting her a killing glance through his quizzing glass.

Damnation, Ravenel thought, clenching his

teeth as he recognized the Honorable Frederic Skeffington. What perverse mischance of fate had planted that empty-headed swell here in East Grinstead at this most unfortunate moment?

" 'Pon my soul," Freddy drawled, sweeping into Gwenda's path, "I heard that Kent is called the garden of England, but I never expected to find a rose amongst the cabbages."

Instead of retreating or even offering the man a chilling stare, Gwenda merely politely requested Skeffington to move out of her way. "You see, I am looking for—"

The dandy smirked. "And you have found him, my dear."

"How could I possibly be wanting to find you? We are not even acquainted, sir."

"That situation is easily remedied."

Ravenel came up between them just in time to prevent Freddy from slipping his arm about Gwenda's waist. "You're going to be in need of a far different sort of remedy, Skeffington," he growled, "if you don't take yourself off at once."

Startled, the dandy drew back, eyeing his lordship from toe to crown through his quizzing glass. "Sobersi—I mean, Lord Ravenel! I thought you were still in London. Well, dish me!"

The baron's hands clenched into fists as he felt himself more than ready to comply with this request. Freddy's gaze settled on his lordship's knuckles, and the young man flushed with dismay, the glass slipping from between his fingers to dangle by its ribbon. "S-steady on, Ravenel, old man. If—if I had had any notion the wench was already bespoken—"

"I am here to escort the *lady* back to her aunt," the baron ground out.

"Her aunt? Oh, quite so." The dandy looked abashed. "I completely misunderstood. I trust you will forgive me, Miss—Miss. . . ?"

But before Gwenda could supply her name, Ravenel took a menacing step closer to Skeffington.

"Yes, yes, I—I'll just be going," Freddy concluded. 'P-pleasant seeing you again, my lord." The dandy took to his heels and fled back to the inn.

Ravenel battled an urge to charge after him and give him the thrashing he deserved. Freddy Skeffington had ever been an insolent dog. At the very least, Ravenel should have drawn his cork and—Suddenly appalled by his own thoughts, the baron allowed his hands to uncurl. What in the blazes was the matter with him? Although he frequently enjoyed a bit of exercise with his fists in the privacy of Gentleman Jackson's salon, never had he come close to doing anything so vulgar as actually engaging in a brawl. He had the feeling that he had just made a complete spectacle of himself. To add to his sense of mortification, he spun around to find Gwenda nearly doubled over with the effort to suppress her chuckles.

"Don't you dare laugh at me." Furiously, Ravenel shook one finger at her. "As usual, this entire wretched scene is your doing, laying yourself open to the advances of one of the most unprincipled rattles in England who—who . . ." His words trailed off, becoming incoherent when she startled him by seizing his hand and pressing it between her own. Her mirth faded; her smile waxed more gentle.

"I wasn't laughing at *you*, Lord Ravenel, " she said earnestly, a soft light coming into her eyes. "I must confess I didn't think that Mr. Skeffington appeared much of a dangerous rakehell, but all the same you were perfectly splendid. No knight charging to the rescue of his lady could ever appeared more fearsome."

"That will do, Miss Vickers. No need to turn this into a scene from one of your novels." The baron hastily disentangled his hand from hers. He was not accustomed to being admired by a lady, and never had any shown a tendency to see him in the role of a knight errant. Rather sheepishly, he had to admit the image was not entirely displeasing.

"You will at least allow me to thank you," she said.

"The best thanks would be if you could contrive to stay out of trouble for five minutes." He attempted to maintain a stern front. "You shouldn't go about risking your reputation by drawing the attention of strange men, especially one the cut of Freddie Skeffington."

"Why? Is he really such a loose screw?"

"You should not use such cant terms, either, but yes. That is exactly what he is and—"

"He did have the most interesting cloak," Gwenda interrupted.

"I was not discussing his cloak, Miss Vickers, but your habit of—"

"You would look well in a cloak like that."

She tipped her head to one side in a thoughtful, considering manner. "Of course, not with such a ridiculous number of capes. Two or three tiers would suffice."

"Miss Vickers!"

"Yes, two capes would accent the width of your shoulders nicely."

Ravenel resisted the ungentlemanly urge to clap a hand over her mouth so that she would be forced to listen to him. "Would you kindly stop changing the subject," he said irritably. "What were you doing out here alone, anyway?"

"I was looking for Bertie. He has run off again."

"That cursed dog! Whose shoe has he pinched this time?"

"No one's. He spotted a cat to chase." She shrugged apologetically. " 'Tis Bertie's other fatal weakness."

His lordship heaved an exasperated sigh. Seizing her by the elbow, he started to propel Gwenda back toward the inn. "You might have asked me to look for the infernal creature instead of waltzing about where you could be accosted by any ruffian chancing through here for a glass of ale."

Although she went along meekly enough, Gwenda voiced a mild protest. "I assumed a spinster such as myself would be safe, especially while garbed in this mousy gown. I am hardly a green girl anymore, you know.

Ravenel snorted. "Miss Vickers, you are just about as green as those eyes of yours. As for that gown, dismal as it is, that sheer fabric does nothing to disguise the fact . . ."

He slowed his step as his gaze was drawn involuntarily to the outline of Gwenda's hips, the tantalizing curve of her bosom. A lovely pink blush stole into Gwenda's cheeks, which only served to emphasize the impression the lady gave of wide-eyed innocence.

Damn! The baron swore under his breath. She would never be safe left on her own. The lady was too heedless, too trusting, and far too attractive. She strolled about with her head poked somewhere in the clouds with little notion of either the conventions or the perils of the real world.

He halted in his tracks, the decision looming up before him like a tangible barrier, the decision that was as inevitable as the payment of land taxes or the occasional visit to the toothdrawer. His shoulders slumped with resignation.

"Come along," he said. "It is high time we returned to the carriage."

"We? " Gwenda asked, angling a surprised look up at him. "You mean to say there is no conveyance for you to hire here at East Grinstead, either? "

"No." Ravenel averted his eyes as he uttered the bald lie. " 'Twould seem I must impose upon your hospitality a while longer. At least as far as Lewes."

Aye, Lewes. There he could hire a rig and follow her the rest of the short distance to Brighton. They would not be seen to arrive together and he could still be sure she was deposited safely upon her family's doorstep, thus satisfying all that conscience, honor, and Jarvis could possibly demand of a fellow.

The baron cut off all of Gwenda's assurance that she would be delighted to have his continued company and hustled her toward the stableyard.

When Jarvis was informed of the change in their plans, he replied in wooden accents, "Very good, my lord." But Ravenel thought the old man had a most disquieting twinkle in his eye as he followed the baron and Miss Vickers toward the coach.

"But what about Bertie?" Gwenda asked, trying to hang back.

"I'll find him. You wait inside the coach. If Skeffington spots us together again and realizes you don't have an aunt, you won't have shred of reputation left."

Gwenda dug in her heels even as her footman moved to open the carriage door. "You should have told Mr. Skeffington I was with my uncle and then Jarvis—"

"Skeffington would have no difficulty in recognizing Jarvis as my valet. *Get in*, Miss Vickers." Ravenel braced his arm about her waist and all but lifted her bodily into the vehicle.

"And don't let her escape," he ordered Jarvis, "before I get back with that blasted dog."

He did not wait for any acknowledgment of his command. He started off at once in pursuit of Spotted Bert. The task did not take him as long as he feared, for he had not gone many steps when Bertie came loping around the side of the stables. But he was obliged to waste considerable precious time removing some burrs from the animal's smooth coat.

"Serves you right," Ravenel muttered as Bertie let out a yelp when one prickly thorn stuck a little deeper than the rest. "Mayhap next time you'll think twice before you . . ." Horrified, he let his words trail off. Damn it, now *he* was starting to talk to the dog in much the same manner as he oft heard Gwenda do.

Ignoring Spotted Bert's licks of gratitude, the baron shooed the animal up onto his perch beside Fitch. Upon second inspection of Miss Vickers's coachman, his lordship decided he was no more impressed with the fellow than he had been earlier. Granted, Fitch appeared a little more relaxed, but his face was flushed and sweaty, his eyes shifting in a most guilty fashion away from Ravenel's when he informed the man they were finally ready to depart.

His sense of unease was not mitigated by noticing that the sun seemed to be slowly vanishing. Gray clouds scudded over the day's previous brightness; ominous shadows darkened on the horizon. If Ravenel's own coachman had been sitting on the box, he would have directed him to spring the horses in order to gain some time before the rain broke. But with Fitch, Ravenel issued a stern admonition for him to drive with care.

"Shurtainly, my lord," Fitch mumbled, tipping his hat with a bovine smile. Then he gathered up the reins, his deep baritone voice breaking into a loud chorus of "The Girl I Left Behind Me."

As the baron took his seat in the carriage, he wondered in what unlikely place the Vickerses had found Fitch, but he was afraid to ask. The coach lumbered down the rutted lane, leaving East Grinstead behind them.

The gathering gloom beyond the carriage windows seemed to cast a pall over their party. They had not gone many miles when Gwenda felt her eyelids growing heavy despite the increased jouncing of the coach. After her drugged sleep of the night before, one would have thought she would feel well rested today. Instead, she somehow waxed more tired than usual. She struggled to stifle a yawn, but it was not easy, especially watching Jarvis nodding off in his corner.

She thought it would be intolerably rude of her to do likewise, but then Ravenel did not seem at all inclined for conversation. He was far too preoccupied with stealing frowning glances up at the sky and checking his pocket watch at periodic intervals.

Nestling her head against the squabs, Gwenda regarded the baron dreamily through half-lowered lids, her mind reverting to the incident in the garden of the Dorset Arms. Ravenel had been a sight to stir any maiden's heart: charging to her rescue with that fiercely protective light in his eyes, every muscle in his formidable masculine frame tensed for battle.

She had never been rescued before, Gwenda reflected with another yawn, had never had reason to be. It would have all been so perfect if, instead of a mincing, ginger-haired fop wielding a quizzing glass, Freddy Skeffington had been a shade more villainous, satanically dark, his cadaverous fingers gripping a twisted dagger. With such thoughts teasing her imagination, Gwenda's eyes drifted closed. . . .

. . . *she was running across the deck of a ship, the tall masts lost in a ghostlike mist, her heart thumping in terror. Hunched beneath his layering capes, Captain Frederici was but a breath behind her. Risking one glance over her shoulder, she saw the glint of the evil pirate's single eye, heard his chilling laugh as his bony fingers reached out to grasp her arms.* . . .

"Oh," Gwenda moaned, slumping down farther on the carriage seat. "Roderigo . . . help me! "

*Even as she struggled in Frederici's cruel grip, another dark form leaped down from the rigging, the familiar scarlet-lined black cloak sweeping back from stalwart shoulders. Strong hands reached out to pluck the villain away from Gwenda, hurling the fiend into the sea. With a glad cry, Gwenda flung herself against her rescuer's chest, burying her face against stiffly starched white linen.* . . .

Gwenda's nose twitched as she mumbled, "Roderigo, what are you doing with that cravat? " Her sleep-smoothed brow furrowed with confusion.

*The mists seemed to part, for once clearly re-*
*vealing to her the features of Roderigo, Count de*
*Fiorelli. She caught a glimpse of a hard angular*
*jaw and cheekbones, a full, sensual mouth, and*
*flashing dark eyes set beneath heavy black*
*brows—all somehow disturbingly familiar. But*
*the next instant his face vanished as the deck*
*pitched beneath Gwenda's feet, the ship heaving*
*in the grip of the storm. Roderigo lost his balance*
*and fell on top of her. . . .*

"Ow," Gwenda breathed, her eyes jerking
open. Wide awake, she was astonished to find
herself still pinned beneath Roderigo's hard-
muscled frame. No, it wasn't Roderigo at all. It
was Ravenel who was struggling to ease his
weight from her—not an easy task considering
the way the coach was rocking and swaying like
a small ketch caught in a tidal wave.

"What . . . what?" she faltered.

"It's that blasted coachman of yours," Ravenel
grated, managing to wrench himself to his feet.
"He's been picking up speed the last half mile or
so." Bracing himself, he strove to help Jarvis,
whom Gwenda suddenly realized lay tumbled on
the floor.

She snatched at the back of the seat to prevent
being tossed about any more that she already was.
From the slant of the carriage, she realized they
must be thundering up a hill at an appalling rate.
Through the window, she obtained a rollicking
glimpse of what seemed a world gone gray.

After hauling Jarvis back onto the seat, Ravenel tried to bang on the coach roof and was

nearly overset on top of her once more. "That fool can't take a hill at such an out-and-out clip," he shouted at her, "or he'll never be able to check the team going down."

"I know that," Gwenda screamed back. "What do you expect me to—oh!"

Her reply was cut off as the carriage crested the hill and started on a mad downward plunge. As Ravenel collapsed on top of his valet, Gwenda lost her grip on the seat and tumbled across the baron's lap. For the next terrifying seconds, she, Ravenel, and Jarvis seem naught but a bruising tangle of arms and legs.

With a muttered oath, the baron shoved her ruthlessly off him. As Gwenda hit the coach floor with a jarring thud, she brushed the hair from her eyes to glare at him.

Ravenel had somehow gained his feet. "Damned fool," he muttered. "Got to do something before he kills us all." His jaw steeled with grim determination, he reached for the coach door.

With a flash of horror, Gwenda realized what he was contemplating. Her heroes often did such mad feats as climbing out of a racing coach to do battle with villains or to halt a runaway, but to see the baron about to attempt such a thing in earnest caused her heart to give a wild leap of fear.

"Ravenel! No—" she started to cry out, but a cracking noise split the air and the coach gave a sickening lurch to one side. The door was flung open, and before Gwenda's terrified gaze, Ravenel lost his balance and pitched out into the blur of dust beyond.

# Chapter 5

Green . . . Ravenel's startled gaze registered a splash of green bare seconds before his body struck the ground. But it couldn't be grass, the ridiculous thought flashed through his mind. Grass couldn't possibly be so—oof!—damned hard.

The impact of his fall drove the breath from his lungs and sent him rolling over and over until he at last thudded to a halt. Closing his eyes tight, he attempted to dispel the black webbing that danced before him, to banish the ringing from his ears. His mind was a blur of confusion, except for the urgent need to draw a gulp of air into his pain-racked chest.

Several shuddering breaths later, the world finally seemed to stop spinning beneath him. He was lying flat on his back and something cold was brushing against his face. Forcing his eyes open, Ravenel focused on Spotted Bert's nose but a fraction from his own. The dog whined, then licked his cheek.

With a low groan, he shifted onto his side and cursed, trying to prevent Bertie from nuzzling his ear. One hand crushed a dandelion. He glanced down at it, his mind yet numbed with shock, trying to make some sense of his surroundings. He appeared to be sprawled in a pasture, marooned in the middle of nowhere with nary so much as a cottage visible or another living thing except Miss Vickers's dog.

*Miss Vickers!* The carriage. Memory sliced through his throbbing head like the cold, sharp edge of a razor. He had been thrown from the carriage just as . . .

Regardless of the pain that spiked along his bruised flesh, Ravenel jerked up onto one elbow, his gaze whipping down the narrow ribbon of dirt road to a point some hundred or so yards distant. His blood froze when he saw the carriage tipped into a ditch, the only figure in sight that fool of a coachman weaving on his feet as he struggled to cut the snorting, plunging horses free of the traces.

But where was Miss Vickers? Jarvis? Dreadful imaginings jolted through the baron, of both the lady and his valet yet trapped inside the coach, possibly bleeding and unconscious. Spurred by panic, he managed to drag himself to his feet. He limped from the meadow with Bertie trailing at his heels.

As soon as he drew near the road, much to his relief, he espied Miss Vickers and Jarvis helping to ease the footman on the grassy bank just above the ditch. James was wailing in a most unmanly fashion.

When Bertie barked, Miss Vickers's head snapped in Ravenel's direction. Releasing her hold on James, she came running down the road, her bonnet flying back, held only by its strings. Ravenel was excessively grateful to note that except for the pallor of her cheeks and the tear at the waist of her gown, she seemed to have no ill effects from the accident. As Bertie raced toward his mistress, the baron paused, expecting that Miss Vickers, overjoyed to find her pet unharmed, would embrace the dog.

He was therefore unprepared when she shoved past Bertie and flung herself against him, the fierceness of her hug nearly sending them both tottering over backward.

"Thank God," she cried, muffling her face against his chest. "I thought you must have been killed."

"Er, yes," Ravenel said gruffly to conceal how moved he was. He could not recall anyone ever becoming distraught over the prospect of his death. There was no doubting the genuineness of her distress. She was making no attempt to weep prettily, as Miss Carruthers would have done. Her breath came in great gulping sobs as she wreaked absolute havoc upon what remained of his cravat. His arms closed about her and he patted her back. "There now, Miss Vickers . . . Gwenda, my dear. Please, you must not upset yourself."

"B-but you terrified me half to d-death." She sniffed. "What—what possessed you to—to try such a mad thing?"

"I will admit it was not the most prudent thing I have ever done," he agreed soothingly. He cradled Gwenda closer, finding the sensation of her soft curves molding against him very agreeable.

But his sense of propriety and responsibility all too quickly reasserted itself. He could scarcely stand here in the middle of the road embracing Gwenda while Jarvis stood anxiously awaiting him, the footman continued to howl, and that dolt of a coachman was doing God knew what to those horses.

Ravenel eased Gwenda away from him. She wiped her eyes with her knuckles, looking a little flustered and mortified by her own tears. "'Twould seem the only one injured is poor James," she said with a quavery smile. "What good fortune we have had."

"A-aye," he agreed, somewhat dubiously, rolling his eyes skyward. If this was Gwenda's notion of good fortune, she was going to be positively ecstatic when those stormclouds gathering over their heads broke. He turned and strode toward the embankment as quickly as his bruised hip would allow.

For a moment Ravenel feared even his stately Jarvis meant to fall upon his neck and weep for joy to find his "Master Des" yet in one piece. But although appearing much shaken, the old man as ever maintained his dignity. Gwenda skirted past Ravenel to bend down beside the footman, who sniveled and clutched his ankle.

Encouraged by Gwenda's murmur of sympathy, James wailed, "Ohhh, 'tis me leg, miss. I've broken it sure."

"Nonsense," she said bracingly. "If you had

done that, the shaft of the bone would likely be protruding through your flesh and—"

Before she could reduce the lad to total hysterics, the baron nudged her aside and made a cursory inspection of James's foot himself. It was not easily done since the footman screeched like a banshee before Ravenel had laid so much as a finger on the injured area.

At last he pronounced, "No, 'tis not broken. Most likely the bone is but chipped, or 'tis a very nasty sprain. As soon as we—"

Ravenel broke off as another squeal pierced the air, but this one did not originate from the unfortunate James. Rather, it was an equine cry of fear. The horses and Fitch. The baron straightened abruptly, beginning to feel a little harried.

He spun about to peer at the front of the upset carriage. Fitch had managed to cut the horses loose, but now as the overexcited animals milled about, the coachman cowered back, wielding his whip as though surrounded by a pack of savage beasts.

"Stop that!" Ravenel bellowed, heading toward the man, but Fitch had already caught one of the leaders on the top of its nose. The horse reared back and then charged down the road, rapidly followed by the other three.

"No! Damnation!" The curse escaped from Ravenel before he was aware of it. Although every muscle in his body shrieked in protest, he leaped down the bank and over the ditch and tore off after the horses. But even if he had been in top form, the pursuit would have been futile. The last horse he had backed at Newmarket should have set such a pace as those four, Ravenel thought bitterly.

He staggered to a halt, clutching his side, and watched their only hope of riding for help vanishing in a cloud of dust. Gwenda drew up breathlessly at his side, holding up her skirts.

"W-well," she said brightly. "At least we know that none of the horses were injured, either. We really have been remarkably lucky. I—I am sure the team will not go far and we will have no difficulty finding them."

The glare Ravenel shot her caused even Gwenda's unquenchable smile to waver. He thought he had held up well until now, considering he was not in the least accustomed to being flung out of carriages or finding his traveling schedule overset by unnecessary accidents. But this last bit of idiocy on the part of the Vickerses' coachman was entirely too much for any sane man to bear.

"Madam," he growled, "if I were a horse, I would flee all the way to hell before I let that cow-handed fool come near me again."

Whipping about, Ravenel advanced on Fitch, his wrath swelling with every painful step. But the coachman showed not the least sign of alarm, not even when the baron seized him by the collar of his driving cape. Rather, it was the baron who recoiled at the heavy odor of stale gin reeking from the man.

Despite the goose egg forming on his forehead, Fitch was obviously feeling no pain. He went limp, directing a muzzy smile past Ravenel at Gwenda.

"Was brave thish time, Mish Vickers," he mumbled. "Took care 'o the 'orses to the lasht."

With that, Fitch rolled up his eyes and sank against the baron in a heap. Ravenel lowered him to the ground none too gently, but the man still curled up on the stone-strewn road as blissfully as though it were a feather bed.

"Oh, dear." Gwenda sighed. "Fitch has shot the cat. Again."

The word *again* went through Ravenel like a cannon blast. "Again?" he asked with a most deadly calm. "Miss Vickers, what do you mean 'again'? Are you telling me that your coachman has a habit of drinking?"

"Well, I would not call it a habit, precisely. But he does like a drop now and again to steady his nerves because . . ." She faltered in the face of his furious stare, then concluded meekly, "Because he's afraid of horses."

"Afraid of horses?" Ravenel said through clenched teeth. It was probably ridiculous to even ask for an explanation, but for the sake of his own sanity, he felt he had to know. *"Then why the blazes did you allow him to drive your coach?"*

"It's rather a long story. You see, Papa organized this musical society and Fitch has the most wonderful baritone for singing catches and glees—"

"Perdition, madam!" Ravenel roared. "Do you people never hire your servants for normal, sane reasons like everyone else does? Did it never occur to your father that a coachman should have some experience, should feel comfortable handling a team?"

Gwenda's chin jutted upward in a defensive manner. "Papa always says that lack of experience should not bar a man from obtaining a situation. If everyone thought the way you do, my lord, how would anyone gain any experience to begin with?"

She sounded so entirely reasonable; it was he who was shouting like a lunatic. That realization did nothing to help Ravenel curb his temper. He raised his hands in a gesture rife with frustration.

"You and your entire family are stark raving mad. And I must be madder still to have ever traveled one inch in your company."

Gwenda flushed bright red, but before she could voice whatever comment trembled on the tip of her tongue, Jarvis appeared, wedging himself between them.

"That will do, Master Desmond," he said sternly, making Ravenel feel all of nine years old again. "I scarcely see that shouting at the young lady will do aught to remedy our situation."

"There is not much else to be done," the baron said, "when here we are, left stranded in the middle of who knows where."

Gwenda bent sideways around Jarvis to glare at Ravenel. "I know precisely where we are. Or—or almost. There is an inn not more than a mile from here. I shall walk there and fetch help."

"Hah!" Ravenel snorted. "You'll do nothing of the kind. Do you think I would set you loose upon an innocent countryside?"

"Master Desmond!" Jarvis looked positively scandalized.

But the baron felt pushed well past the brink of civility or any kind of gentlemanly behavior. Considering the condition of the coachman and James's injury, it was patently obvious to him who would be obliged to go trudging in search of aid. But Miss Vickers hotly refuted the suggestion.

"You? You could not possibly find the place. I have only the vaguest notion myself and would have no way of giving you directions."

"And *this*," Ravenel sneered, "from the woman who declares she knows precisely where we are."

As Gwenda bristled with indignation, Jarvis quickly interposed, " 'Twould seem that the most sensible solution, my lord, would be for you to escort Miss Vickers—"

"I should as lief be escorted by Bertie," Gwenda said.

The baron also voiced his own objection to this scheme. "No, Miss Vickers must stay with you, Jarvis. Do you expect me to leave you alone to cope with one man injured and another drunk?"

Jarvis drew himself up to his full dignity. "I have been coping with all manner of disasters since well before you were born, Master Desmond. But if you now think me such a feeble old man, mayhap it is time I served you notice."

Ravenel bit back an oath. To add to all the other disasters, now he had offended Jarvis. He paced a few furious steps down the road, experiencing a discomfiting feeling of having no control over the situation. At last he conceded with bad grace, "Very well, I shall take you with me, Miss Vickers—"

"How utterly noble of you," Gwenda interrupted in a voice dripping sarcasm.

"—because I am sure Jarvis will be far safer if I do."

"Why, you—you—"

But his lordship did not give Miss Vickers a chance to think up a name bad enough to call him. He moved quickly, dragging the inert coachman off to the side of the road. He examined the wrecked carriage to see if it would prove steady enough to provide some sort of shelter and then settled Jarvis and James inside, making them as comfortable as possible. With a mighty heave, he managed to thrust Fitch's unconscious form onto the coach floor.

He paused briefly in the midst of these exertions to warn Gwenda, "We are going to have to hasten. The next we know, we shall be caught in a thunder shower."

"It is not going to rain," she said loftily. "I have seen those sort of clouds frequently before. They may threaten all day, but the storm never breaks until well after dark."

An hour later, Ravenel, Gwenda, and her dog were yet shuffling wearily down the road, the woodland thickening around them and overshadowing their path.

The baron hunched down, drawing up his collar. "It is starting to rain, Miss Vickers," he informed her in long-suffering accents.

"I am perfectly aware of that, my lord," Gwenda snapped, feeling one large drop splash and trickle down the back of her neck. Even Bertie's tail drooped, the water starting to bead on his glossy black-and-white coat.

Gwenda, accustomed to meeting the direst of calamities with a philosophical good humor, felt more cross than she could ever remember. Step after wretched step they had traveled, with no sign of the inn or the village she had sworn was there. Ravenel said nothing, but from his grim expression she knew it would be only a matter of time before she was treated to another of his long homilies on her scatter-brained ways. Her anticipation of this did little to soothe her temper.

She wrapped her arms about herself as the rain started to come down harder, shivering with the knowledge that she would soon be soaked to the skin. Ravenel stripped off his coat. But the gallant gesture was somewhat diminished by the manner in which he thrust it at her.

"No, thank you," she said. "After everything else, I should not like to have you blaming me if you get a chill."

She gasped when he seized her by the arm and halted her in the middle of the road. He roughly whipped his coat about her shoulders. When she started to discard it, he caught her hand.

"Miss Vickers. Attempt to remove that frock coat and I shall not be answerable for what I might do. Until I met you, I would have sworn that I would never shout at, curse, or strike a lady. You have already provoked me into the first two. . . ." He let the sentence trail off in ominous fashion.

With two brothers Gwenda had learned long

ago not to allow herself to be bullied, but Ravenel made a most formidable figure towering over her. Some elusive memory tugged at her as she studied the piercing light in his dark eyes, the rainwater glistening on his swarthy skin, his wet garments outlining the stalwart set of his shoulders like some storm-swept buccaneer. Then, with a jolt, she realized what it was. Dear heavens, Ravenel looked just like Roderigo had in her recent dream. Or had it been that Roderigo resembled Ravenel? Either way, it was a most disconcerting discovery to make at this particular moment.

"Thank you," she grumbled, allowing the coat to remain around her shoulders. "But, in the future, I wish you would have the goodness to stay out of my dreams."

The baron looked startled, but to Gwenda's relief he merely shook his head and did not question the strange comment she had let slip. As they resumed their trek, he lapsed into this own dark thoughts. After a time, Gwenda saw his lips move as though he were counting something.

"If you have aught to say"—she winced as she trod in a puddle, the water seeping inside her already damp slipper—"I wish you would just say it. It is an odious habit of yours—thinking so loudly."

"I was merely making a tally, Miss Vickers. In the last twenty-four hours I have witnessed the loss of six horses and two carriages. It staggers the imagination."

"*My* carriage is not lost! I know exactly where it is."

"Just as you knew exactly where this elusive inn was to be found."

"We might have stood some chance of finding it if you had let me inquire at that farmhouse we passed awhile back." The miserable way in which Gwenda's sodden skirts were beginning to cling to her legs inspired her with an unreasonable urge to shift all the blame for their trouble on to Ravenel.

"It is peculiarity of men I have frequently noticed," she said. "You can never bear to ask directions or admit when you are lost."

The baron slicked back his rain-soaked dark hair. "At that farmhouse all you would have achieved was the farmer's wife setting her dogs upon us. We are not precisely the most reputable-looking couple, Miss Vickers."

As Ravenel plodded along, he drew himself rigidly upright. Gwenda set her teeth, knowing what was coming.

"If you had not been so insistent in the first place that you knew the way, I would have felt more of a need to make inquiries. But then it is all of a piece with your manner of conducting a journey, ill-conceived and ill-advised—"

"Kindly do not start doing that again!" Gwenda stomped her foot, which had the effect of pelting them both with an additional spray of water.

"Doing what?" his lordship demanded.

"Lecturing me in that pompous manner. It is another annoying habit of yours. Anyone would think you—you were some aged grandsire tyrannizing over a flock of unruly grandchildren."

"Not grandchildren, Miss Vickers, but as the head of my family I do have responsibility for many dependents, younger cousins whom I frequently have had to *lecture*, as you put it."

"*That* must make them all positively dote on you."

Ravenel flinched as though she had hit upon some painful point, but the expression was so fleeting she might well have imagined it. She nearly regretted her spiteful remark, but he quickly recovered himself and began to intone, "One's duty is not always pleasant, either for—"

"Oh, do stop! You are beginning to remind me of Thorne again."

Ravenel shot her a questioning glance from beneath his rain-drenched brows.

"My eldest brother, the most holy, the most God-fearing Reverend Thornton Vickers. Jack and I always call him Thorne because that's what he was—a thorn in our sides, forever prosing on and tattling on us. It is very irritating to be in the company of someone who always considers himself so superior."

Even in the gloomy half light, Gwenda could see how Ravenel flushed. Although he appeared chagrined, he said, "I suppose you think I should find that comparison unflattering. But it so happens I do not. It is most heartening to hear that at least one member of your family is respectable. Where does Reverend Vickers hold his living?"

"He doesn't have one anymore." A hint of wicked satisfaction crept into Gwenda's tone.

"Thorne ran off to become a Methodist. He does most of his preaching in sheep pastures these days."

Lord Ravenel made no effort to stifle his groan.

"Aye, even Thorne is but another one—" What had his lordship called her family earlier? "—one of the *raving mad* Vickers," Gwenda filled in, somewhat bitterly. "I daresay you think the whole lot of us ought to be locked up in Bedlam."

The baron hunched his shoulders, looking uncomfortable, but his jaw squared stubbornly as he replied, "Even you must confess that your family does not exactly march in tune with the rest of the world."

"I thank God that they don't!"

"And that any sort of common sense, notions of propriety, or a well-ordered existence—"

"In my family, enthusiasm and dreams and . . . and imagination have always been valued above your odious common sense. As for your stuffy notions of order, they don't seem to have done much for you. You are one of the most unhappy, bad-tempered men I have ever encountered."

"I had not the least problem with my temper, Miss Vickers, until I—"

"I know! Until you met me." Gwenda choked, an unaccountable lump rising into her throat. She had never felt the need to defend herself or her family before. But his lordship's critical attitude was beginning to raise doubts in her own mind about the delightful skimble-skamble household in which she had been raised, doubts that were far more dampening to her spirits than the rain weighting down her skirts.

His lordship drew up short. "Well, my *odious common sense* tells me we may as well turn back. There is obviously nothing down this road but more trees."

"There is nothing back the way we came, either." Gwenda stubbornly kept on going. When she became aware that Ravenel was not following, she turned to glance impatiently at him. She was annoyed to see that Bertie had halted as well, hanging about his lordship's heels. Even when she called his name, the disloyal hound refused to come to her.

"We are turning back, Miss Vickers," Ravenel said. "We need to find some sort of shelter immediately. I thought I heard thunder just now, and if lightning starts up, I don't care to be walking anywhere near you."

He had said worse to her, but for some reason this last comment brought an unexpected moisture to Gwenda's eyes that had naught to do with the rain. "What a p-perfectly mean thing to say." She whipped about so that he would not see her foolish tears. "You may do as you please, my lord. But *I* am going on."

Gwenda had scarcely taken more than a half-dozen steps when she heard him coming after her. She dashed rain and salt water from her eyes, then stiffened, fully prepared to resist if he attempted to turn her about by force. To her astonishment, he merely proceeded to arrange his coat more firmly about her—a ridiculous gesture, for the garment was as sopping as her gown beneath.

"You are right, my dear," he said softly. "It

123

*was* mean. I have been behaving in a most boorish fashion and I do beg your pardon."

Gwenda tried to harden her heart against him, but it was difficult to do so when the harsh planes of Ravenel's face were gentled by the hint of warmth in his eyes. As she falteringly accepted his apology, she found that she could not meet his gaze. He astonished her further by tucking her arm firmly within the crook of his and guiding her down the road with as much solemn gallantry as though they were taking a stroll through St. James's Park. Although the rain descended upon them in even harder gusts and a threatening rumble of thunder shook the sky, Gwenda experienced a strange feeling of being warm and secure.

Then, as if by some kind of fairy's magic, when they rounded the next bend of the road, she espied the outlines of a building set back amidst the trees.

"Ravenel, there it is," Gwenda said excitedly. "The inn I told you about." Her spirits soared as she felt vindicated. She had been leading the baron in the right direction all the time.

She was pleased to see his lordship looking considerably heartened. Giving her hand a squeeze, he said, "My dear, dear Miss Vickers. Pray forgive my ever having doubted you. May wild horses tear me in two if I ever cast aspersions upon your judgment again."

She giggled when, despite the rain beating down upon them, he paused to sweep her a mock-gallant bow, exhibiting a playful side to his nature that she would never have dreamed he possessed. For once Ravenel seemed to share her feelings of being nigh giddy with the relief of seeing their ordeal about to come to an end, with the prospect of a warm fire, a dry shelter, and a place to rest aching feet.

Linking arms once more, Gwenda and Ravenel splashed through the puddles like a pair of rowdy urchins. Bertie raced ahead of them, barking, showing more frisk than he had the past mile and more. Gwenda's mood of exhilaration did not abate until they slogged through the mud of the yard itself. But as she glanced about her, her heart slowly sank with dismay. This was not any inn she had ever patronized and she found herself wishing she was not about to do so now.

The tumbledown stables appeared fit for nothing but sheltering the most spectral sort of horses. Far from the comforting bustle to be found at the White Hart, not so much as one carriage, one groom, or one ostler was to be seen. The puddle-soaked yard appeared so deserted that Gwenda jumped at the loud banging of a stable door. Her flesh prickled with the uncanny sensation of being watched. And Bertie, her friendly-to-a-fault Bertie, emitted a low growl from his throat.

She all but flung herself against Ravenel's chest when the inn itself was illumined by a jagged flash of lightning. If she had been designing a roost for bandits or a home for wayfaring ghosts, or even conjuring up an isolated spot for murder to be done, her imagination could not have produced anything that would rival this place. It was a most decrepit-looking Tudor structure: the wooden beams projected an aura of decay, the mullioned windows glared like baleful dark eyes. The inn sign creaked in the wind, its chipped paint depicting a scantily clad prizefighter, its faded letters proclaiming *The Nonesuch.*

Ravenel eased Gwenda away from him. The rain pelted his face as he tipped back his head to glance at the sign and she could tell he had already forgotten his recent vow not to cast any more aspersions on her judgment. His whole manner was one of insufferable resignation, as though he had been expecting all along that she would bring down some fresh calamity upon his head.

"It is much more congenial on the inside," Gwenda said, feeling her defensive hackles start to rise.

She watched the baron reach for the wrought-iron door handle and had to fight back an urge to stop him. But what could she say? That the Nonesuch gave her a very bad *feeling*? Ravenel would only fancy her a bigger fool than he already did. She had no choice but to suppress her forebodings.

The rusted iron hinges screeched like an evil bird of omen as he thrust wide the inn door.

# Chapter 6

*. . . the castle walls, cold and bleak, closed about the Lady Emeraude like a well of doom. The stones themselves seemed wrought of evil, mortared with the blood of innocents, weathered by fingers plucking at them in despair. . . .*

"Miss Vickers! You are cutting off the flow of blood through my arm."

The baron's protest jarred Gwenda out of her imaginings. She suddenly realized how tightly she had been clutching him as they crossed the threshold of the Nonesuch.

"S-sorry." She forced herself to release him, then nearly tripped over Bertie, who bounded in ahead of her. As his lordship slammed the door closed behind them, she thought she knew how her poor heroine Emeraude must have felt when thrust into the evil Armatello's lair. Gwenda resolved never again to treat her heroines so shabbily.

Not—she was obliged to admit—that the taproom before her resembled in the least the Gothic splendors of her villain's gloom-ridden *castello* except perhaps in its starkness. The inn's walls were unadorned but for some bits of cracking plaster; the taproom housed an oak bar counter and a few crude tables and rough benches. A feeble effort at a fire smoked and hissed upon the blackened stone hearth. The logs had been recently kindled and were yet damp, Gwenda judged, from the way they crackled. The room was unoccupied, but along the far wall a door stood ajar.

"Hallo!" Ravenel called. "Is anyone within?"

His inquiry was met with naught but the rain lashing against the windows.

"No one is here," Gwenda whispered. She looked for some sign that Ravenel shared her uneasiness, but his lordship merely appeared annoyed that his summons had not been answered forthwith.

"Of course someone is here," he said. "That fire did not build itself."

What an unfortunate way of putting it, Gwenda thought. She envisioned a pair of disembodied hands stacking the wood. That was one of the dreadful things about having a lively imagination, she had long since discovered. At times, it could be most inconvenient. She could not restrain a shiver that had little to do with the wet gown clinging to her skin.

"Come over by the fire," Ravenel said. "You are soaked through."

"As if you are not!"

But he ignored her retort. Showing no concern for his own discomfort, the baron proceeded to remove his drenched coat from her shoulders. His strong fingers untied the wet strings of her bonnet, then tugged it from her head, brushing aside the damp tendrils of hair from her forehead.

"There. Now mayhap you can start to dry out a—" Ravenel broke off as Bertie shook out his coat, spraying them both with a shower of droplets.

"Blast that dog!" But there was more of exasperated tolerance in his lordship's voice than any real anger. Gwenda noted with astonishment that the irascible Lord Ravenel was accepting this latest disastrous turn of events with much better humor than either she or Bertie.

While her dog suspiciously snuffled one of the benches, Gwenda's eyes roved about the room, coming to rest on the mantel where a large, sinister spider was about to feast on the blood of a beetle caught in its webbing.

" 'This place has an aura of evil about it,' " she said, quoting the heroine of her last book, " '. . . an odor of death and decay.' "

The baron sniffed the air and crinkled his nose. "That's frying onions," he said. "I'll check the kitchens for the landlord."

Before he could stir a step, Bertie suddenly flattened back his ears, a deep-throated growl escaping him. Gwenda resumed her grip on Ravenel's arm as the door at the end of the room began to creak open slowly.

She sent up a silent prayer that the Nonesuch's landlord would prove to be a round, jolly sort of fellow like Mr. Leatherbury. Even better, he might have a plump, apple-cheeked wife to fuss over Gwenda and chase all these nonsensical fears out of her head.

. But as the host made his appearance, wiping bony hands on a soiled white apron, she let out a quavery sigh. It could not be worse than if she had strayed into one of her own novels. With stooped shoulders, a hooklike nose, squinty eyes, and coarse black hair, the wretch might as well have had "villain" inscribed all over his sallow skin.

"What's toward—" he started to snap with a heavy frown but was cut off by Bertie. The dog charged forward, barking and baring his teeth.

"Eh! Get back, you flamin' brute." The man retreated and snatched up a cudgel from behind the bar counter.

"No! You monster!" Gwenda cried, rushing forward as he threatened to bring the heavy wood crashing down upon Bertie's head. "Don't you dare!"

But Ravenel moved faster, catching hold of Bert's collar and dragging the snarling dog back out of harm's way.

"Down, Bertie!" Ravenel thundered. "Quiet!"

Spotted Bert stopped barking but continued to growl. The hair at the back of his neck bristled as at the next instant a set of whiskers emerged from behind the bar. A fat black cat tore off for the kitchen at a waddling run.

The host stepped forward, brandishing his cudgel at all of them. "Clear out! The pair of you and take that slaverin' beast with you afore I bash his skull."

If Gwenda had had any misgivings about the

Nonesuch and its host before, Bertie's reaction to the man only served to confirm it. "We shall be only too happy to do so," she said, reaching for Bertie's collar.

"No we won't," Ravenel said, although he released the dog to her care. "I have no intention of being thrown back out into the storm."

He turned the full weight of his formidable stare on the landlord. "If this is how you treat your customers, I am not surprised to find your establishment empty."

"I'm closed t'dy," the man grumbled, but he lowered the cudgel. "And I never have aught to do with beggars."

"We are not beggars but victims of a coaching accident," Ravenel said in his most lordly tones.

"What's that to me? I don't repair coaches here. Be off with you."

"We are not seeking repairs, my good man, but a place of shelter. Then I need some horses and a coach to be sent to fetch the servants and baggage we were forced to leave behind. The lady and I will require some dry clothes, and later, a bit of supper."

Gwenda, struggling to keep a grip on Bertie, blinked at the baron in astonishment. He rapped out his commands as though he truly expected this surly rogue to obey him.

*"Lady?"* The man's squinty eyes flicked over Gwenda. "That's rich, 'pon my word."

Ravenel moved so quickly that Gwenda scarcely had time to gasp. He wretched the cudgel from the host's hands and fairly lifted the weasely fellow off his feet by his collar. It took all of Gwenda's strength to restrain Bertie, who seemed eager to join his lordship in the assault.

"The lady," the baron repeated with stony emphasis. "My sister, Miss Gwenda ... Treverly, and I am Lord Ravenel. We are both accustomed to being accorded a little more respect."

Although the man's gaze roved fearfully up the baron's towering length, he choked out, " 'Twouldn't matter if you was the Prince Regent hisself. There's naught I can do for you. This inn is closed."

"Mayhap I can persuade you to open it." Ravenel released the man. The host staggered, one bone-thin hand snaking up to rub his unwashed neck. His lordship groped for his waistcoat pocket. He took great pains to display both the chain of his gold pocket watch and the ruby signet ring he wore as he drew forth a thick wad of damp bank notes and flicked them.

Gwenda made a small sound of protest, which went unheeded. She could not believe the sensible Lord Ravenel could be so foolhardy. Did he not see the gleam of greed in that villain's eye? Did he not notice the furtive licking of the lips? Scarcely realizing what she did, she bent down beside Bertie and huddled the dog protectively closer.

With a feeling of dread, she noted the immediate change in the host's manner. Rubbing his bony hands together, he whined, "Well, there might be somewhat I could do. Never let it be said that Orville Mordred turned his back upon fellow creatures in distress."

"Mordred? His name would be something like

that," Gwenda muttered into Bertie's ear. The dog growled as though in agreement.

Mordred scratched his long, pointed chin. "Happen to have an ostler I could send off with my own rig to fetch your servants."

"Good. Make arrangements to do so at once." Ravenel complacently returned the money to his pocket, seemingly blind to all of Gwenda's efforts to catch his eye. "And if you have a woman on the premises who could attend to my sister . . ."

"Alas, no, there isn't." Mordred attempted an ingratiating smile that revealed two brown stumps where his front teeth should have been. "My missus was called away unexpected-like to her mother in Leeds."

More likely he murdered his wife and stuffed her up the chimney, Gwenda thought. That's why it doesn't draw properly. Feeling that she had kept silent for far too long, she straightened and cleared her throat.

"M-my lord." Belatedly, Gwenda remembered the relationship the baron had bestowed upon them. "Brother dear, might I have a word with you?"

Ravenel looked startled, then quickly recovered himself. "Oh. Er, certainly, my dear sister."

As he approached, Gwenda caught him by his wet sleeve and tugged him closer to the fire. She stole a glance at Mordred. Although the man appeared nonchalant enough, she could have sworn the villainous rascal's ears grew by several inches in an effort to hear what she whispered to the baron.

Gwenda kept her voice so low, Ravenel was

obliged to bend his tall frame to the point where the curve of his cheek was but a breath away from her lips.

"Lord Ravenel, I—I must tell you the truth. This was not the inn I was looking for. I have never been to this place in my life."

"I rather guessed that, my dear." The baron's brief smile would have been intolerable if not for the unexpected gleam of tender amusement in his eyes.

Her pulse gave a little flutter, but she ignored the sensation as she whispered urgently, "We—we cannot stay in this dreadful place. That fellow is likely plotting to slit both our throats."

"Miss Vickers! This is not the time to let your imagination—"

" 'Tis not my imagination. You have only to look at that man to see what a scoundrel he is." She gestured vigorously to where Mordred leaned against the bar, feigning to remove some of the dirt from beneath his nails with a small jackknife. "He has mean eyes and," she added, as a triumphant clincher, "Bertie growled at him."

Ravenel sighed with weary patience. "Bertie was growling at the cat."

"He was not! That was not Bertie's cat-chasing growl. He—" Her protest was cut off by Ravenel's laying his fingertips upon her lips.

"I perfectly agree with you, Gwenda," he said gently, lowering his hand. "I am sure Mordred is a rogue, but the worst I anticipate is his charging me thrice for whatever miserable service he offers."

"But—"

"And we have no choice. The storm shows no sign of abating and I am worried about Jarvis and the others with only that broken-down coach for shelter."

"Oh. A-aye, the others," Gwenda said in a small voice. A guilty flush mounted into her cheeks. She had been so caught up in her own apprehensions, she had nigh forgotten the unfortunate circumstances in which they had left James, Fitch, and the baron's elderly valet.

Ravenel's hand enveloped hers in a reassuring squeeze. "Trust me. Everything will turn out all right."

Gwenda trusted him completely. It was Mordred she had her doubts about. But his lordship was correct. They had no choice.

When the baron turned back to the landlord, Mordred straightened immediately, all servile attention.

"I'll have a look at that carriage of yours now," Ravenel said, "as soon as my sister is settled into a private parlor."

"Alas, my lord, we don't have such a thing here. But I would be only too pleased to let the young lady have the use of my missus's sitting room."

All traces of his former insolence gone, the host could not have been more cloyingly polite. But as Mordred flashed her a crocodilelike smile, Gwenda thought she by far preferred it when he was surly. As the man bowed her through the open doorway, she was reminded of the large black spider yet busily spinning its web on the mantel.

Mrs. Mordred's sitting room proved a most curious chamber, small and narrow. The cozy homespun rug, overstuffed horsehair sofa, and battered tea table were jarringly at odds with the collection of blunderbusses and muskets mounted upon the wall. The sight of these weapons made Gwenda wish she had had the foresight to bring along her own pearl-handled pistol.

The baron eyed the room with great disfavor but muttered, "Well, at least there is a better fire here than in the taproom. You stay close to the hearth and try to get some of the dampness out of your dress. I will not be gone long."

"Of course," she said dolefully. Here Ravenel was, preparing to leave her alone in the very heart of a murderer's den, and he was worried she might be taking a chill. But Gwenda managed to put up a brave front, not wishing the baron to think her a complete ninnyhammer.

Only when the door had closed behind his lordship did she rub her arms and glance about her with a tiny shiver. Bertie was restless, too, sniffing in every corner. He seemed to be particularly fascinated by an old pianoforte shoved against the wall. When Gwenda drew tremblingly closer to investigate, she saw that the dog had discovered nothing more than a mouse hole. Next to it was a large workbasket, presumably Mrs. Mordred's.

She must be a strange sort of woman, indeed, for beneath the stack of sewing Gwenda could just make out the top of a bottle of gin. Her mind began to conjure up images of guilt-ridden consciences, murders ages old, mayhap someone walled up alive in the chimney bricking, a family accursed, the present generation driven to madness and strong drink.

With a tiny sigh, she located a small three-legged stool and ensconced herself on it by the blazing logs on the hearth. There was naught left for her to do but wait for Ravenel and allow her imagination to run riot.

The baron stood in the inn doorway, anxiously drumming his fingers as he watched the Nonesuch's ancient coach lumber out of the stable-yard, vanishing behind dark sheetings of rain. Never in his life had he found himself in such a quandary. He had longed to return with the coach and seek Jarvis out himself, but it would have been unthinkable to drag Miss Vickers back out into the storm or to abandon her in such dubious quarters as the Nonesuch.

At least the groom Mordred had produced from the stable had seemed a sturdy, sensible fellow, kindly despite his rough accent. But in this foul weather, even if the groom carefully followed the directions given him, Ravenel could not expect to see the carriage return with Jarvis within the next few hours.

And even if Mordred could be persuaded to hire out the vehicle, it would be close to midnight before the baron ever deposited Miss Vickers safely in Brighton. A heavy frown creased his brow. Who was he trying to fool? There was no possibility of traveling any farther this day. No matter what time the carriage returned, his elderly valet was certain to be done in by the afternoon's events, and there was also the footman's injured ankle to be dealt with. No, he might as well face the fact. They were all going to have to spend the night in this wretched place.

As Ravenel closed the door, shutting out the patter of the rain, his soft curse echoed about the empty taproom. Miss Vickers might be fretting and conjuring up all sorts of faradiddles about their host's murderous intent, but she obviously failed to see the true nature of their predicament.

They were apparently the only guests at the Nonesuch, she without any sort of chaperone or female traveling companion. If it ever became known—and experience had taught Ravenel that such mishaps usually had a way of leaking out—there would be the very devil of a scandal. Her reputation would be utterly ruined.

Not that it was in any way his fault, the baron thought, but it was not precisely hers, either. The lady could not help it if she had been born a Vickers, taught to hire baritones for coachmen and French trollops for maids. But, blast it all, no Baron Ravenel had ever been involved in scandal, and he was not about to be the first. If he had to, he would even . . .

He clenched his eyes tight, a shudder coursing through him. No! He could not possibly be thinking of *marrying* Miss Gwenda Mary Vickers.

"Your lordship?"

Ravenel's eyes flew open to find Mordred at his elbow. The fellow did have a most nasty manner of creeping up on one. The baron had not even heard him enter the taproom.

"What is it?" Ravenel snapped.

"I was only wanting to know if I should be preparing a room for your lordship . . . and your sister?"

The baron battled an urge to smack the suggestive leer from the man's face. It was obvious the innkeeper had not believed the sister-brother Banbury tale. But, then, who would? Ravenel wondered gloomily, his shoulders sagging.

"No. That is . . . yes. We will require *two* rooms—one for myself and my valet, another for the lady."

The man's eyebrows rose even in the face of Ravenel's challenging stare, then Mordred merely shrugged and went to carry out his lordship's bidding, leaving Ravenel to find his own way back to the sitting room.

Just beyond the taproom, a pair of rickety stairs led up to the second floor. In the corridor beyond the stairs, he saw two doors but could not quite remember behind which one he had left Gwenda. He tried the first one; the handle would not turn. Before he could apply more force, he heard Bertie's bark in the opposite room. He supposed this particular door led to the kitchens or the cellar, but how strange that Mordred should keep it locked.

The baron felt far too preoccupied to give the matter more than a passing thought. As he strode toward the other door, his mind revolved with schemes to render his situation with Gwenda innocuous, more proper, to find some way to spare her reputation without sacrificing his own sanity.

But at the moment his brain seemed too numbed with weariness to function clearly.

Rubbing his brow, he pushed his way into the sitting room. Gwenda sat huddled near the fire, her bedraggled skirts appearing to have reached the same state of semidamp discomfort as his own garb.

Bert yipped with joy to see Ravenel, but his lordship discouraged any warmer tokens of welcome. He forced the dog to lie down on the rug before turning his attention to Gwenda. Faced with the prospect that this woman might well have to become his wife, Ravenel found himself studying her more intently than he had ever done before. Of course, Gwenda could scarcely be expected to be looking her best under the circumstances. But that was the curious thing. The baron, who had ever preferred a lady to be neat and precise, thought that Gwenda had never looked more charming than now, when her face was framed by a riot of chestnut curls drying into the most tousled disorder. The heat from the hearth had brought a becoming blush of rose into her cheeks; her green eyes reflected the gold of the firelight. The velvety outline of her mouth was enough to invite any man to—

Ravenel checked his thoughts when Gwenda's gaze shifted in his direction, almost as though she had felt the weight of his stare. He flushed guiltily, then rubbed his hands together in a too hearty manner.

"Well, the coach is on its way," he said in what he felt was the most foolish manner possible. After all that had passed between himself and

Gwenda, why was he suddenly feeling so awkward with her, so acutely aware of their situation . . . alone . . . together. To conceal this inexplicable attack of nervousness, he stomped about, blustering, "That rogue Mordred has not done one thing to see to your comfort. He could at least have managed a cup of tea."

Although Gwenda protested she wanted nothing, Ravenel flung open the sitting-room door and bellowed for the innkeeper. But his summons was answered by a youth who identified himself as Rob.

"Mis-ter Mordred . . . bade me . . . wait . . . upon you . . . and the lady," Rob intoned, like a child who has been taught to say his piece by rote.

The lad both looked and smelled as though his customary place was in the stables, but nonetheless the baron asked what the inn could offer by way of a supper.

"L-leg of mutton . . . fried rabbit . . . spitchcock eel," Rob recited.

Ravenel did not feel as though he could quite face a spitchcock eel, but he put in an order for the mutton. Gwenda did not appear to notice what was taking place. She was so unusually silent, he felt his own sense of discomfort increase. As soon as the boy had scurried out of the room, Ravenel stole another furtive glance at her.

He noticed the fear shading her eyes, the way her hands trembled. Of course. She, too, must at last be realizing the nature of their plight. He cursed himself silently for an inconsiderate fool. So caught up in his own feelings, he had given no thought to what Gwenda's must be. Besides worrying about the prospect of her own ruin, she might well be harboring other terrors. After all, their acquaintance was brief. She might be supposing him the sort of bounder who would take advantage of this situation.

A rush of tenderness surged through him, a protective urge to draw her onto his lap and . . . No, what was he thinking of? That would scarcely be likely to reassure her.

Instead, Ravenel pulled up another stool beside her and reached for her hands. Despite the fire, they felt slightly chilled.

She gazed at him, her brow furrowing. "Oh, Lord Ravenel, I have been thinking. . . ." Her lashes swept up so that he was staring full into those ever-changeable green-gold eyes. He wondered if it really would be such a terrible fate to have to wed Gwenda Mary Vickers.

"Yes?" he prompted gently when she hesitated.

"Do you . . ." Her voice quavered. "Do you believe in ghosts?"

"Do I what!"

This question was so far from anything Ravenel had expected that he was torn between an urge to shake her and to laugh aloud. He released her hands, saying tartly, "I have never given the matter of ghosts much thought."

Gwenda's eyes shifted fearfully about the room. "What would you do if one were to rise up before you this very minute?"

"I would tell it to go away. I object to being haunted before I have had my dinner."

A reluctant smile quivered upon her lips,

drawing forth the most appealing dimple. "Aye, I daresay you would."

Ravenel could see clearly what had been taking place in his absence. When Gwenda should have been agonizing over the prospect of her social ruin, the same imagination that had fashioned the terrors of *The Dark Hand* had been busily at work instead.

Before the baron could scold Gwenda for her nonsense, a timid knock sounded on the door. It was Rob returning to lay covers on the tea table. Ravenel was relieved to see that although Bertie sniffed at the lad's thick hobnail boots, the dog did not take the same exception to Rob that he had to Mordred. Gwenda, however, was another matter. She regarded the stable boy with an expression of horror.

When the lad had gone, she turned to Ravenel and gasped, "You couldn't possibly be thinking of eating anything!"

"Well, yes. That was largely my intent." His lordship lifted the cover off one of the dishes. The mutton looked overcooked, but he suddenly realized he was famished. He had had nothing to eat since breakfast.

When he invited Gwenda to join him, she vigorously shook her head.

"You must suit yourself, my dear," Ravenel said, too weary to coax her and too exhausted to stand on ceremony. He sat down at the table, but before he could raise one bite to his lips, Gwenda rushed across the room and all but snatched the fork from his hand.

"Don't! It might be poisoned."

"Gwenda—"

"No, truly! Pray listen to me, Lord Ravenel. There are worse possibilities than ghosts. I have heard of obscure inns where the unwary are lured in and poisoned or clubbed over the head . . ."

The baron leaned back in his chair with an exasperated sigh. "We were not lured in. The landlord did his best to get rid of us."

"That's exactly what I mean," Gwenda said, making his head nigh ache with her vehement illogic.

Still, he might have humored her and set aside his plate, no matter how hungry he was, if he had believed her to be genuinely distressed. But he detected a certain sparkle in her eye and began to suspect that she actually enjoyed terrifying herself with all these imaginings.

He wrestled his fork from her grasp and stubbornly attacked the food on his plate. But it was difficult to eat with any great relish with Gwenda on one side of him, looking as though she expected each mouthful to be his last, and Bert on the other, regarding him with pleading canine eyes.

Ravenel's appetite rapidly diminished. He flung down the fork in disgust and lowered his plate for Bertie, who devoured the remainder in two great gulps. The baron then had to spend several minutes convincing Gwenda that he had not just poisoned her dog.

The only tolerable part of the meal was the surprising quality of the brandy, which Rob served after clearing the dishes away. Ravenel had a hard time persuading Gwenda to let him drink it, but the struggle was well worth it. He had not sampled such fine spirits since he had drunk the last bottles he had been able to obtain from France.

He wished Gwenda would toss off a bumper herself. It would do her a world of good, help her to relax. Ravenel feared if he did not soon give her something else to think about besides ghosts and murderers, she would drive him to distraction. If her mind worked in the manner of an ordinary sort of young lady, he would not have to be racking his brains for some way to make her understand the real problem that faced them. As it was, he could think of no easy way to introduce the unpleasant subject.

He set down his brandy glass and took to pacing the narrow room. Unfortunately, Gwenda did the same and they frequently had to come to abrupt halts to avoid colliding. The only one behaving sensibly, Ravenel noted wryly, was Spotted Bert. The dog yawned and watched their progress from a cozy spot where he was curled up before the fire.

Ravenel stalked over to the windows, the sky pitch-black beyond, but at least the rain had nearly ceased. The carriage sent to rescue Jarvis would likely return soon. That would be a great relief, but it scarcely did anything to alter the situation with Gwenda. The baron glanced over his shoulder and noted that the lady had paused in her perambulations long enough to poke the fire.

How would she react when he told her she would likely have to marry him? Gwenda was so unpredictable, there was no telling. Scarcely thinking what he was doing, he hovered nervously near the pianoforte. He didn't realize he had begun to plunk out a tune on the keys until Gwenda replaced the poker and exclaimed in surprise, "I didn't know you played. I—I mean, I never fancied that *you* would—"

"I don't." Ravenel flushed, quickly drawing back his hand. "That is, I never had lessons. I play a little by ear."

"But what a remarkable talent to waste. Why did you never have a tutor?"

He shrugged his shoulders in a manner that was a shade too offhand. A childhood memory he had thought long forgotten surfaced in his mind: the stern uncle who had been his guardian actually locking the door to the music room at Ravenel so that the baron could not succumb to temptation.

He unconsciously repeated his late uncle's words. "Playing the pianoforte is not something the Baron Ravenel is expected to know."

"But—but if you are fond of music . . ." Gwenda faltered, looking thoroughly confused.

And so she would be, Ravenel suddenly realized. He could almost hear her saying again, "In my family, enthusiasm and dreams and imagination have always been valued above your odious common sense."

He suppressed a strange twinge of envy as he tried to explain to her, "My being fond of music is all the more reason I should avoid it. A man in my position cannot afford foolish distractions."

He did not truly expect Gwenda to understand this point of view, but neither was he prepared for the sympathy that shone so warmly from her eyes.

It both embarrassed and disconcerted him. Why the deuce should she be feeling sorry for him, when it was she who was hovering on the brink of social disaster? He said gruffly, "There are far more pressing matters for you to worry about than my lack of music lessons, matters that do not seem to have occurred to you."

"Such as?"

"Such as the fact that we have been pitchforked together in the most devilish manner. "You and I—we . . ." To his annoyance, Ravenel felt his face growing red, his tongue seeming to tie itself in knots.

"We what?" Gwenda asked, crinkling her nose.

Her air of innocent bewilderment snapped the last of his patience. He crossed the room and roughly seized her upper arms. "Damn it, Gwenda. You have to marry me."

Her eyes widened; her mouth dropped open. She had never found her imagination lacking before, but not even in her wildest dreamings had she ever thought of Ravenel clasping her in such a passionate manner, demanding that she be his wife. Nor had she imagined what her own reaction would be. She blushed. She trembled. Her heart pounded so loudly she could scarcely hear her own tremulous breathing.

"Oh, Roderi—Ravenel," she stammered. "I—I never dreamed that—that you would feel this way."

"Of course I would. I am a man of honor, after all."

"So you are," she murmured shyly. "My chivalrous knight."

"I could scarcely just ride away after I had compromised you, no matter how unwitting it was on my part. As a Ravenel, I could not tolerate that sort of scandal."

The hand that Gwenda had been reaching up to stroke the rugged line of his lordship's cheek froze in midair. "What?" she asked faintly. "What are you talking about?"

He shot her a look more impatient than loverlike. "My dear, you will be utterly ruined if it is known you spent the night at the same inn as I, unchaperoned. That is why I have no choice but to marry you."

The rose-lined cloud upon which Gwenda floated dissolved from under her feet. Ravenel did indeed bear a most heroic cast to his countenance at this moment, but it was more of the nobility of one about to bravely embrace a firing squad than his lady. She squirmed free of his grip.

"Oh. I see," she said dully, surprised by the keenness of her disappointment. "How—how utterly *honorable* of you. But as a Vickers, I didn't think you believed I had a reputation worth saving."

The baron looked momentarily shamefaced, but he recovered himself. "We are not discussing any remarks I might have made previously about your family. When we are wed, I assure you I would not be so ill-bred as to utter any further criticisms. No matter what should happen, I would never be so uncivil as to blame you—"

"Please." Gwenda groaned. "Do not start making any speeches. You presume entirely too much, my lord. I have no intention of accepting your *generous* offer."

"I was not offering. I was telling," he said, his voice rising with every word. "You have to marry me. As a Ravenel—"

"Exactly whose good name are you trying to protect?" she interrupted acidly. "Yours or mine?"

"Yours! If you but had the wit to know it. And though I do not expect you to feel in the least grateful."

"Grateful!" Gwenda's own voice became successively more shrill. The sound of their quarrel roused Bertie enough so that he opened one eye to regard them sleepily.

She shouted, "How dare you talk of gratitude when you inform me you must marry me, with your face looking grim as death."

"Forgive me if my manner offends you," Ravenel bellowed back. "But in the past eight hours, I have been thrown from a carriage, nigh drowned in a thunderstorm, given indigestion from overcooked meat—"

"I told you not to eat it!"

"—which is not calculated to put a man in the most gallant frame of mind."

Gwenda rubbed her arms where her flesh had recently felt the strong pressure of his fingers. "Well, I will say one thing," she flung out. "At least this proposal is somewhat of an improvement over the one you made to Miss Carruthers."

The dangerous spark that flared in Ravenel's eyes should have caused Gwenda to fall silent. But Thorne had always told her that her besetting sin was never knowing when to hold her tongue. She continued, "I would never marry you, not even to save my reputation. No, not even if I was to be branded for a trollop and dragged to the pillory tomorrow."

A muscle twitched along Ravenel's jawline. He approached her with an ominous deadly calm that was far more devastating than any outright show of anger. Gwenda had enough sense to retreat behind the tea table.

"So you would never marry me?" he hissed in accents of soft menace. "I daresay you don't find me romantic enough. A most boring, stuffy man."

"I—I did not mean that, precisely," she said, wondering exactly what he intended to do when he got his hands on her.

"Old Sobersides Ravenel. Not in the least like any of those dashing heroes you write about."

"I—I never said that."

Indeed, if Ravenel only knew how exactly like one of her heroes he did look at this moment, stalking her around the tea table in his weather-stained white shirt, his undone cravat revealing the bronzed flesh of his neck, his dark eyes raking her in a manner that both threatened and tantalized. How often had Roderigo appeared thusly in her dreams, only moments before he would attempt to bestow upon her that elusive kiss that never seemed to materialize.

Gwenda stopped in her tracks, tracing the sensual outline of Ravenel's mouth with her gaze. What was she doing? Here might be the perfect opportunity to find out about that kiss, and she was nearly flinging it away by retreating. But no. She blushed to the roots of her curls. What a scandalous notion! She couldn't possibly demand of Ravenel a thing like that. But if she didn't, she might never in her life have such another chance.

The words seemed to spill from her lips of their own accord. "Ravenel. Have—have you ever kissed a woman before?"

"Have I—" Her question brought him to an abrupt halt, bare inches between them. "Of course I have." He added bitterly, "Though I daresay you'd tell me I don't do that right, either."

"I have no way of judging unless you do so."

Despite his angry mood, Ravenel looked a little taken aback.

"And you can hardly expect me to marry you unless you kiss me first," Gwenda said, entirely forgetting that she had just told him she would never marry him on any account.

Ravenel appeared far more likely to box her ears. But he grabbed her by the shoulders, hauled her forward, and planted a kiss on her lips that was swift, hard, and far from satisfactory. But as he was pulling back, their eyes met and some lightning awareness seemed to spark between them.

He drew her into his arms more gently this time. Gwenda came without resisting until she was pressed so close to his chest, their bodies seemed to melt together. His head bent toward hers, his hand cradling the back of her neck. The moment stretched out forever, as in one of her dreams, and as Gwenda stared deep into the night-dark pools that were Ravenel's eyes, she was certain she would wake too soon, as she always did.

But then his mouth covered hers, tenderly at

first so that she could savor the warm texture of his lips. Gwenda tried to capture her feelings at this moment, but it was impossible. As Ravenel deepened the kiss, all thought sifted through her mind like quicksilver until she held no memory of aught save Ravenel and the wondrous, fiery sensation of his lips on hers.

He pulled back, his mouth parting from hers with a lingering reluctance. His voice was husky. "My—my dear Gwenda. I should not. I am taking the most shameful advantage of your inno—"

"Don't waste time apologizing," she begged. "Just kiss me again." She flung her arms about his neck. Ever a quick study, Gwenda proceeded to demonstrate to Ravenel just how much she had learned from their first embrace. She pressed her mouth to his in an ardent kiss that was even sweeter, headier than the last one had been. Ravenel crushed her hard against him, returning her passion with fervor, when suddenly he wrenched himself free.

"Miss Vickers!" he gasped. This time it was the baron who retreated around the tea table. When Gwenda murmured in protest and attempted to follow him, he held up one hand to ward her off.

"No, no more of that," he said, panting. "Not until we are married."

She could not tell whether he appeared more shocked by his own behavior or hers. The warm glow enveloping her faded, leaving her overcome with feelings of shame and misery.

She pressed her hands to her flaming cheeks. "We are not getting married. I—I have been kissing you under false pretenses . . . b-because you look like him and—and he looks like you. I never knew how R-Roderigo ought to kiss before, but I never thought . . . And how could one begin to describe such a devastating experience in a book, anyway?"

Since she concluded this rather incoherent speech by bursting into tears, it did not surprise her that Ravenel should look thoroughly confused. He kept a most wary distance between them.

"We are both more than a little overwrought from the day's events," he said. "You should retire. I'll just go and inquire if your room is ready, and we'll settle this matter in the morning." The baron spun on his heel and retreated briskly from the room.

" 'Tis s-settled now! I am not m-marrying you," Gwenda cried, but the door had already closed behind Ravenel.

Bert stood up, stretched, yawned, and ambled over to nuzzle Gwenda's hand sympathetically. She gave a doleful sniff and patted the dog. "Oh, Bertie! If he had any doubts before, now I have thoroughly convinced him that I am a lunatic." She stomped her foot. "As if I give a fig for his opinion or his beastly honorable proposals!"

She wiped her eyes angrily on her sleeve and managed to compose herself by the time his lordship returned with the young waiter, Rob, bearing a candlestick to light her way.

Ravenel bade her a curt good night and promised to have her trunk sent up as soon as it arrived. "And be sure to keep your door locked" were his final words to her, before retreating to the fire and presenting her with the rigid outline of his back.

Gwenda glared at him through her tears and followed Rob from the sitting room, Bertie trailing after them. As they mounted the creaking stairs to the upper floor, the candle flame cast eerie, flickering shadows upon the inn's ancient, gloom-shrouded walls. Under other circumstances, she would have permitted herself a delicious shiver, allowed her mind to conjure up all sorts of sinister images. But at the moment her thoughts were too full of the recent tempestuous scene with Ravenel.

The boy indicated the door to the chamber that was to be hers, but when she moved to sweep past him, Rob suddenly blurted out, "His lordship never said a truer thing!"

"What?" Gwenda asked sharply, wanting only for the boy to be gone so that she could be alone.

"About keeping your door locked, miss." Rob leaned forward, lowering his voice to a frightened pitch. "And not venturing out of your room tonight, not under any circumstances."

It was the kind of dire warning she had often used in her books, but she scarce heeded the sense of what Rob was saying.

"Of course," she said, giving the boy an impatient, weary smile. Taking the candle, she whisked into her chamber and fairly shut the door in Rob's anxious face.

## Chapter 7

"That woman *is* going to marry me," Ravenel muttered, clenching his jaw to an almost painful state of stubbornness.

"Of course, my lord," Jarvis said. He had lost track of the number of times he had uttered that soothing phrase since his arrival at the None-such a half hour ago. Never had he seen his young master in such a pelter. From what few mumbled words he caught, Jarvis supposed his lordship to be fretting over Miss Carruthers and her rejection of him. But why, in the wake of everything else that had happened, should such a thing now be preying upon Master Des's mind? The only likely explanation was that his lord-ship was overwrought. It behooved Jarvis to get him into bed as quickly as possible.

The valet rolled back the coverlet and eyed the sheets with great disfavor. Yellowed, thread-bare, they appeared apt to come apart at the slightest touch. He clucked his tongue. "This bed is very likely full of vermin, my lord."

"Good," his lordship replied in abstracted

fashion. "Make sure there are at least two. I shall never get to sleep otherwise."

Jarvis swiveled his head to stare at Ravenel in astonishment, then realized that his lordship had scarce heeded a word said to him. By the light of an oil lamp, its glow obscured by a dusty globe, his lordship pawed through one of his trunks. He found his dressing gown, which he proceeded to don inside out.

You have had a very long day, Master Des, Jarvis thought. He had been worried about his lordship and Miss Vickers ever since he had watched the young couple vanish down the road and saw the rain coming on. But his anxieties would have been tenfold worse if he had known they had fetched up in this dirty, tumbledown inn.

"It would have been far better if I had come and rescued you, my lord." Jarvis could not help voicing this opinion for mayhap the dozenth time. A grunt was his only reply.

Jarvis felt he had fared much better than Lord Ravenel and the young lady. The rain had barely begun when a farm cart had happened by. If only they had known there was a snug cottage within walking distance a bare quarter of mile beyond the field where his lordship had been flung.

After hailing the cart, Jarvis had soon had the drunken coachman and the poor young footman comfortably settled in the cozy farmhouse with plump Mrs. Ladbroke fussing and plying them with hot tea. With her help, Jarvis had bandaged James's ankle and sobered up the coachman. Jarvis would have been well content if not for his nagging fears over Lord Ravenel's continued absence. When the carriage from the Nonesuch had arrived in search of him, Jarvis had been most eager to leave. Not so Fitch or James, he thought with disapproval. They were too self-ishly concerned with their own ailments to stir a step for their mistress. These young servants nowadays. It would have taken more than a sprained ankle or a raging headache to keep Jarvis from Master Des.

Through all this Jarvis was a trifle ashamed to feel a twinge of smugness. The young master oft seemed so sure his poor old valet was beyond coping with any disaster. Jarvis thought he had done rather well today, shown his lordship he was not completely past it. Had he remembered to tell Master Des with what foresight he had left a note pinned inside the wrecked carriage, otherwise the groom from the Nonesuch never would have found him at Mrs. Ladbroke's cottage?

"Yes, Jarvis. You told me. Several times," was his lordship's disgruntled reply.

While Ravenel took to pacing again, Jarvis hunted for a warming pan to take some of the dampness from the sheets, then he thought better of it. Any friction would likely cause that worn linen to disintegrate entirely.

The baron brushed past him, grumbling under his breath, "Blasted woman. Not one grain of common sense beneath all those curls. But I know my duty."

Jarvis paused in his efforts to plump up the pillows to study Ravenel anxiously. It was always a bad sign when the master began to pace. And was the look in his eye a trifle feverish?

"I trust you have not taken a chill, my lord."

"No, Jarvis," Ravenel said with barely concealed impatience. A permanent frown appeared creased between his brows.

If not ill, Jarvis concluded, the master was in a devilish bad skin over something ... something more than all these traveling mishaps or the conditions of this dreadful inn. Jarvis knew his lordship and Miss Vickers had not set out today on the most amiable terms with each other. Still, Miss Vickers was such a good-natured young lady. Jarvis could not believe she had plagued his lordship with either tantrums or hysterics.

He cleared his throat and ventured sympathetically, "It has been a most trying day, my lord. I daresay you and Miss Vickers had a monotonous time of it, waiting here at this rundown inn."

"Monotonous!"

To Jarvis's surprise and alarm, Master Des halted in his tracks and emitted a bark of wild laughter. "No, Jarvis. Miss Vickers might inflict many torments upon a man, but monotony would never be one of them."

The words were no sooner out of Ravenel's mouth than he wished he had returned a more noncommittal answer. Jarvis was regarding him with renewed uneasiness, the scrutiny of his still keen blue eyes probing deep enough to render the baron mighty uncomfortable. He felt himself coloring and returned to rummaging through his trunks, demanding what had become of his tooth powder.

Jarvis located it for him in a trice. "I am glad to hear my lord was not bored. I trust you at least passed your evening with some degree of comfort?"

The valet's concern and curiosity irritated Ravenel's taut nerves to the snapping point. He straightened, brandishing his toothbrush. "If you must know, Jarvis, Miss Vickers and I spent our time inspecting the food for poison and waiting for ghosts to whisk down the chimney. That is, when we weren't engaged in shouting matches and chasing each other 'round the tea table."

To say nothing of the kissing, he added to himself, an embarrassing flush of heat rushing through his loins at the memory. And to think nothing of it, either, if he wished to get any sleep at all tonight.

He continued, scarce giving Jarvis time to register his dismay. "But I suppose these events will become everyday occurrences when Miss Vickers and I are married. I shall soon grow to regard them as commonplace."

If he had expected to shock the imperturbable Jarvis, Ravenel was disappointed. Although the old man exclaimed, "Marry Miss Vickers?" he appeared more worried than startled. "But, my lord, what about Miss Carruthers?"

"Miss Carruthers? What the deuce does she have to do with any of this?"

"I thought that you were wanting to marry her only yesterday morning."

Yesterday morning? Ravenel marveled. Aye,

so it had been, and yet the scene with Miss Carruthers seemed as hazy in his memory as though it had taken place in another lifetime. The only part that remained clear to him was bending over that settle and finding tumbled brown curls, abashed green eyes, a pixieish smile. Was it truly only yesterday that Gwenda Mary Vickers had erupted into his life? It seemed more like years since he had last bade good-bye to a sane existence.

He said curtly, "I asked Miss Carruthers and she turned me down. So now I am going to marry Miss Vickers."

Jarvis's fine white eyebrows jutted upward in disapproval. "Miss Vickers is indeed a charming young lady, but 'twould seem your lordship's decision is rather sudden."

"Damnation, Jarvis. You of all people should understand why I am doing this. Honor demands it. I could scarcely allow her reputation to be ruined owing to this little escapade."

"Is not your lordship being a trifle rash? Chances are that matters might be arranged so that no one would ever know about this mishap."

Ravenel found himself unexpectedly irritated by Jarvis's well-meant comments. "No, the affair is quite hopeless. I must marry her, and that's flat."

"And what is Miss Vickers's opinion?"

As usual, Jarvis had an uncanny knack for cutting through to the heart of the matter. The baron thought of Gwenda's insistence that she would never wed him, and his mouth set into its former obstinate line.

"Miss Vickers's impractical opinions are of no consequence. She has no more choice than I. I will make her marry me. I see my duty quite clearly."

With that, Ravenel flung down his toothbrush. There was no water in the chipped porcelain basin, anyway. He stalked toward the bed, the silence into which Jarvis had lapsed becoming more unnerving with each passing second.

"Well?" Ravenel rounded on his valet. "You never liked Miss Carruthers in any case. So are you not going to wish me joy?"

"Not yet, my lord." Jarvis's cryptic remark and sudden smile were both equally annoying. Ravenel decided he had had all he could possibly endure for one day.

When Jarvis helped him out of his dressing gown, he flung himself into bed. Catching the edge of the sheet, he gave it an angry jerk and rolled over in accompaniment to the sound of tearing linen.

"I am not going to marry that overbearing man, Bertie," Gwenda declared to her dog, who was attempting to arrange himself on the window seat. Silhouetted against the glass, Spotted Bert issued a mournful whine like some hound of dire prophecy.

Beyond the latticed panes, the moon made a ghostly glow cresting the night-beclouded sky. Upon the nightstand, a candle burned low in its socket. A draft whistled past the window, causing the flame to waver, sending shadows leaping up the dark-paneled walls of the chamber.

Amid the moth-eaten velvet splendor of the bedcurtains, Gwenda tossed and turned on the lumpy feather-tick mattress. The room must once have been the finest the Nonesuch had to offer, but now its decay was worthy of any ruined castle whose mortar had ever dripped from the ink of Gwenda's pen.

The door didn't latch properly, either. Gwenda had discovered that earlier when she had answered a timid knocking. It had been Rob bringing up the trunk with her meager belongings, which Jarvis had had the forethought to see recovered from the wrecked coach. After the lad had gone, Gwenda had realized there was no way to lock the door, leaving her prey to whatever might be creeping abroad tonight in the corridor.

Never in her life had she so much scope for her imagination to run rampant, and never in her life had she been so indifferent to it all.

Despairing of ever finding a comfortable position, she sat bolt upright in bed, hugged her knees to her chest, and complained, "Ravenel might have delivered the trunk to me himself. Along with an apology. The effrontery of the man, Bertie! The insufferable condescension. As though he were doing me the greatest of favors. The high-and-mighty Lord Ravenel stooping to wed one of the half-mad Vickers. As if I would ever consider his odious proposal."

Did she fancy it or was there a rather accusing gleam in Spotted Bert's eyes? Gwenda squirmed. "Well, I might have been carried away for just an instant. When he first spoke of marriage, he seemed so much like I had envisioned Roderigo."

Gwenda closed her eyes and touched a trembling finger to lips, yet tasting of the fiery passion of Ravenel's kiss. She groaned. "Ohhhh! How can any man so—so positively stuffed with duty, honor, and pomposity possibly kiss that way?" She pummeled her pillow in frustration. "It isn't fair, Bertie. It simply isn't fair."

She ceased the assault when she saw some of the feathers flying out.

Bertie gave a soft, reproachful bark. He crouched down on the seat, burying his head beneath his paws almost as though trying to shut out some of her grumblings.

"I do beg your pardon, Bertie," Gwenda said bitterly. "Pray excuse me for having troubled you with my trifling problems." She rolled over with one last parting shot. "But I'm not going to marry that man. I'll be hanged if I do."

She drew the musty coverlet up to ears, but with such thoughts churning in her head, it was some time before she drifted off to sleep. Even then it was a most restless slumber, with disturbing snatches of dreams.

*She stumbled through the mist-obscured ruins, pursuing an elusive, ever-familiar stalwart figure garbed in a black cape. . . .*

"Roderigo," Gwenda groaned into her pillow. "Wait for me, my love."

*Running so fast, her heart seemed ready to burst. She could never quite catch up to the raven-*

*haired man or make him hear her. Then, as from
a great distance, she heard . . . barking?*

Gwenda tossed from side to side. Bertie! What
was he doing here at the castle?

*Her dog was growling, attacking the edge of the
dark-cloaked man's cape. Gwenda staggered forward, begging Bert to stop. No! Heel, Bertie, heel!
It is Roderigo. It is . . . The man turned slowly
around. It was Lord Ravenel. His strong arms
reached out for her, the sensual curve of his lips
curved into a mocking smile, the dark glow of his
eyes seeming to mesmerize, to draw her on. . . .*

"Stop it," Gwenda mumbled. "You are not
Roderigo. You are not."

It took every ounce of resistance she possessed
to wrench herself awake. She sat up, breathing
hard, brushing back damp tendrils of hair from
her eyes.

"Damn that man, Bertie!" she gasped, directing her gaze toward the window seat. "I told him
. . . I did—"

She broke off, her words faltering. Although
the candle had long ago guttered out, the pale
glow of the moon was enough for her to realize
the window seat was empty. Gwenda groped
about in the darkness, expecting to find Bert
curled up at the foot of the bed, but her hands
encountered nothing but the rumpled coverlet.

It was then she noticed the shard of light slic-
ing its way across the floor, light that emanated

from the crack where the door to her bedchamber stood ajar.

Gwenda's hands tightened on the sheet as she hugged it to her breast.

"B-Bertie?" she called softly. There was no answer. She called louder, a little more urgently. "Bert!"

Still no response. But it was nothing to be alarmed about, she tried to assure herself. Bertie was frequently given to nocturnal wanderings. He might have scented that black cat again or—Gwenda grimaced at a less comforting thought—or Mordred.

Shivering, she swung herself out of bed. She located her wrapper and tugged it on over her nightgown. Padding cautiously to the door, she peeked out. There was no sign of Bert or anyone else in the corridor beyond. But someone had left a candle burning in the old-fashioned wrought-iron wall sconce.

"H-here, Bertie." Gwenda tried to whistle, but she was so nervous she couldn't pucker. A heavy thud issuing from the lower story of the inn nearly caused her to jump from her skin. The noise was followed by the unmistakable creak of footsteps.

It must be well past midnight, she told herself. Yet someone was up and stirring. Someone or *something*.

She swallowed hard, trying to ignore the uncomfortable pounding of her heart.

"Blast you, Bertie," she whispered, wishing the dog was safe in her room, wishing her room had a bar a foot thick. Her gaze traveled wistfully toward a closed door only two down from her own room—the door that Rob had informed her earlier led to Ravenel's lodging.

But no. Gwenda could well imagine what the baron's scathing comment would be if she roused him in the middle of the night to go searching for Spotted Bert. As if she needed his lordship's help in any case, she thought, stiffening her spine.

She was sure Bertie hadn't gone far. Most likely that was him she heard below in the kitchens, knocking things over, making a nuisance of himself.

"W-won't I give him a dreadful scold when I find him," she said with a quavery laugh. Of course, Ravenel was right about one thing. There was not the least reason to be frightened. The Nonesuch was naught but a neglected old building.

All the same, Gwenda first took the precaution of fetching her pearl-handled pistol from the trunk. She set it to one side while she searched for something to put on her bare feet, pleased to find that for once she had not mislaid her slippers. Shoving her feet into the soft leather, she stepped out into the hallway. With trembling hands, she removed the candle from the sconce and used it to light her way down the stairs.

The wretched steps did have to creak so, shrieking her approach to whomever might be lurking— No. Gwenda set her lips resolutely. She could not allow herself to think such ridiculous things. There was no *whomever*—only Bertie.

When she reached the lower floor, she raised

the candle and glanced nervously about. All seemed quiet and yet . . .

The darkness itself, the inn's very walls seemed to have taken on life. The hair prickled at the back of Gwenda's neck. She could feel a presence, eyes watching her.

Then she heard another floorboard creak—and she hadn't moved. "Oh, Bertie," she quavered. "Please let it be you."

But the prayer had scarce left her lips when a hand shot out of the shadows behind her, gripping her shoulder. Gwenda screamed and spun about like one demented. She flailed the candle before her like a sword, spattering hot wax on her knuckles.

The light flickered across Ravenel's brocade dressing gown as he flung up one arm to shield his face. "Damme, Gwenda! Stop that before you set me on fire."

"R-Ravenel?" Gwenda sagged back against the wall, just barely managing to steady the candle while she pressed her other hand over the region of her wildly thumping heart.

His lordship cautiously lowered his arm. "What the deuce are you doing here, Gwenda?"

"What am I— What are *you* doing creeping up on me in that fashion? 'Twas enough to send me into a fit of apoplexy."

"I could not sleep. I went into the taproom to see if I could find a spot more of that brandy." His lips compressed in a stern manner that by now Gwenda found all too annoyingly familiar. "Now, madam. You will please account for your own presence."

All traces of Gwenda's recent fright faded before a rush of anger. She said, "If it is any of your concern, Lord Ravenel, I am looking for my dog."

"The dog be damned! I will not have you chasing about this place in the dead of night garbed only in your bed clothes. Go back to your room at once."

"I will do no such thing." Gwenda bristled at his proprietary tone. The temerity of the man. He behaved as though he were already her husband. In any case he was a fine one to talk of being garbed only in night clothes. 'Twas obvious that beneath his robe his lordship wore naught but his breeches. The opening in the brocade revealed glimpses of a hair-roughened chest. Gwenda had the grace to blush when she realized she was staring at the contours of his muscular frame a little too intently.

"Are you not afraid of encountering any cutthroats, or worse, down here in the dark?" Ravenel asked, a wicked glint coming into his eye.

Gwenda could see clearly what he was about. If he could not bully her into obeying his commands, he meant to frighten her. She raised her chin defiantly. "I am not in the least afraid. After all, I have . . ." Her haughty words faded to silence as she groped with one hand in the pocket of her wrapper and found it empty. She had been so pleased with herself for remembering her slippers, she had forgotten the pistol.

Her face flushing with chagrin, she lowered her gaze. Not about to admit her absentmindedness or her qualms to Ravenel, she declared stoutly, "Now if you will excuse me, I am going to find Bert."

She spun on her heel, and marched down the hall, but she immediately heard Ravenel coming after her.

"I will find the wretched animal," he began.

"No, thank you. I want no more of your *chivalrous* gestures."

Gwenda paused outside the door that led to the kitchens and reached for the handle.

"Of all the ridiculous notions. You'll never find him in there," the baron said. "I tried that door earlier and it is kept locked."

When the handle turned easily in Gwenda's grasp and the door creaked open, she could not forbear shooting him a look of triumph. She herself doubted that Bertie had come this way, but she was not about to give Ravenel the satisfaction of admitting that.

Tiptoeing into the kitchen, she sensed him close behind her. As she softly called Bertie's name, the light from her candle spilled over a grease-laden iron stove stacked high with dirty pots that looked as if they had not been cleaned at any time during this century. A plump rat stood sampling something from an unwashed plate, but when the light fell upon it, it quickly vanished behind the stove.

Gwenda shuddered. "And to think you actually ate something prepared in here," she could not refrain from reminding Ravenel.

He grimaced, but all he said was, "I hope you are satisfied. You can see Bert is not here. The sensible thing for you to do is—What the deuce!"

He broke off, staring past her with an arrested expression on his face. Gwenda glanced somewhat nervously behind her to see what had caught his attention.

It was the door that led into the kitchens from the yard outside. It was flung wide open, the night breezes and pale moonlight contriving to make sinister rustling shadows of the trees beyond.

"There's something out there," Ravenel muttered.

"Bertie?" Gwenda asked weakly, feeling her heart begin to sink down to her toes.

"I don't think so. Give me the candle, Gwenda."

She did as he asked but whispered anxiously, "What for?"

"I am going to see what's out there."

This notion seemed so far removed from Ravenel's usual good judgment that Gwenda started to protest, but his lordship was already striding purposefully forward. He flung a curt command to her to remain where she was, but she took no heed of that and followed, clinging to his arm. She could feel the tension cording his muscles, making them whip-taut.

"Gwenda, I told you— Damme!"

She heard Ravenel crack his knee against something, then he staggered, nearly oversetting them both. When he regained his balance, he bent to rub his leg, cursing softly. Then he held the candle so as to illumine the object that had blocked their path.

Gwenda stared in frowning surprise at a pile

of small wooden casks piled willy-nilly just inside the kitchen door.

"What is it?" she breathed. "Gunpowder?"

The baron made a closer inspection of one of the kegs, then a slow smile spread across his face. "No, not gunpowder, my dear. Brandy."

"Brandy!"

"Aye," he said. "I don't wish to alarm you, Gwenda, but I believe we have stumbled upon a bit of smuggling."

Far from being alarmed, Gwenda was flooded with a sense of keen disappointment. "Smuggling? Is that all?" she asked.

"I am afraid so, my dear."

"And, after all my lovely conjectures about murders and—and family curses and ghosts!"

Although Ravenel regarded her solemnly enough, Gwenda had the curious impression that he was being hard-pressed to maintain a straight face. "Mayhap we had better—"

But Gwenda never knew what Ravenel was about to suggest. A tall shadow suddenly loomed in the kitchen's open doorway. Gwenda gave a terrified gasp and dove into Ravenel's arms. She could feel his own heart give a lurch as he tensed to confront the intruder.

But the moon-silhouetted figure on the threshold appeared as alarmed as Gwenda.

"Oh, lordy," Rob yelped, nearly dropping the cask he was carrying as Ravenel directed the light from the candle full in his face.

For several seconds, none of them moved. As Gwenda caught her breath, she watched Rob's Adam's apple bob up and down.

"Miss. Y-your lordship," he stammered. "You shouldn't be down here." He set the cask down with a dull thud.

"Neither should you," the baron said pleasantly enough, although Gwenda felt him tighten one arm protectively about her waist.

"I—I—was just doing a bit of work for Mr. Mordred," the lad said, twisting his hands. "M-moving some molasses down into the s-storeroom."

"Molasses, indeed. More like smuggling a bit of brandy."

They might well have been the king's soldiers, Gwenda thought, about to clap irons upon the unfortunate young man from the way Rob's teeth began to chatter.

"Oh, no, m'lord! 'Twarn't me. Me and Mr. Mordred don't do no smuggling. 'Tis old Tom Quince that does that and he—he brings the stuff up from the coast for us just to pass 'round the neighborhood."

Gwenda squirmed away from Ravenel to lay one hand reassuringly on the boy's arm. "Goodness. Don't put yourself into such a taking. We weren't spying on you—only looking for my dog."

"Oh!" Rob's expression of relief was quickly replaced by a furtive one of guilt.

"Have you seen the dog, lad?" Ravenel asked.

Instead of answering, the boy hung his head. Gwenda felt a sudden squeezing of fear inside her.

"Rob, what has happened to my dog?"

"Nothing so terrible," Rob mumbled. "B-but Mr. Mordred—he made me do it."

172

"Do what?" Gwenda cried.

"Well, you see, miss, your dog came sniffling around outside and when he saw Mr. Mordred—he went for him. Dogs don't seem to like Mr. Mordred noways. Your Bert . . . he took quite a chunk out of Mr. Mordred's leg—"

"Astonishing," Ravenel interrupted. " 'Twould seem that hound does possess some sense of discrimination."

Gwenda gave him a reproachful look before prodding Rob. "And then?"

"I had to do something, miss, or Mr. Mordred would have shot the dog sure. I tied him up in the stable, and to keep him quiet I—"

"Tied him up!" Gwenda exclaimed, allowing Rob to explain no further. Why, Bertie had never been so abused in his life. Never had he been thus confined. She could well imagine what poor Bert must be feeling: confused, terrified at being shut up in those dark stables.

"We've got to let him out at once," she said indignantly. She shoved past Rob and was halfway out the door when Ravenel caught her roughly by the arm.

"Are you mad?" he asked. "You can't go charging out there. There's a band of smugglers creeping about."

"Only two," Rob interposed. "Mr. Mordred and old Tom Quince. But truly, miss, it would be better to wait until morning."

Gwenda might well have been persuaded, but at that moment a low, piteous howl carried from the direction of the stables.

"Bertie!" she cried. "Don't be afraid. I'm coming."

Wrenching free of Ravenel, she tore off, running around the side of the inn and heading for the stableyard. Mud splashed against her legs from the puddle-soaked yard, but she had no thought for anything but rescuing her dog. Gwenda heard the baron's furious hiss as he came charging after her, but she, far lighter on her feet, managed to outdistance him.

Not stopping to draw breath, even when she reached the stables, she drew aside the bar and flung wide the heavy door. Bursting inside, she found Bert cowering in the first empty stall. His moist eyes gleamed up at her through the dark. He whined, attempted to stand, and then flopped back on his haunches.

"Bertie! What have they done to you!" Gwenda dropped to her knees in the straw and flung her arms about him. Bert's head sagged against her chest.

Ravenel burst through the stable door. He paused a moment, gasping, before starting to scold, "Gwenda, you little fool—"

"Bertie is hurt." She cut him off, choking on a half-sob. "He cannot even stand."

The baron frowned and knelt down beside her. Bertie squirmed with his usual delight to see his lordship. But when he attempted to greet him, the dog's head lolled to one side. Bertie's tongue shot out to lick Ravenel's cheek and missed.

The baron sniffed the air and then grimaced. "Damnation. That boy must have given Bert some of the brandy to quiet him. The dog's not hurt. He's as drunk as your coachman."

"Don't be ridiculous. Bertie couldn't possibly—" Gwenda recoiled as the dog panted in her face and she smelled it, too: the reek of strong spirits.

"Oh, Bertie," Gwenda groaned. The dog regarded her muzzily through half-closed eyes. "Whatever am I going to do with him, Ravenel?"

Ravenel got to his feet, dusting wisps of straw from the knees of his breeches. "You will simply have to let him sleep it off."

"I'm not leaving him tied up here in the stables! Not with that dreadful Mordred likely to come back." Gwenda began struggling with the knot of the rope looped around Bertie's neck, a difficult task in the semidarkness.

The baron caught her by the elbow and tried to haul her to her feet. "I will take care of Bert, Gwenda. But I want you to slip back to your room before someone catches . . ."

He allowed the sentence to trail off at the sound of a heavy footfall just outside the stable door. The next instant light flashed into Gwenda's eyes, momentarily blinding her. She heard the sharp intake of Ravenel's breath. Stifling her own shocked outcry, she saw that it was Mordred. He walked with a pronounced limp, his breeches torn presumably by Bertie's teeth. In one hand he held a horn lantern, in the other an upraised pistol. The baron stepped in front of Gwenda so that the muzzle was aimed directly at his chest. He mentally cursed himself for a fool. At the first hint of anything amiss, he should have forced Gwenda back to her room.

"You two!" Mordred blanched with dismay, then spat in disgust. "I might have known. I should have chased the pair of you and that damned dog back into the storm. But my generous nature is always getting the better o' me. I had a bad premonition about letting you stay."

Despite how pale and frightened she looked, Gwenda inquired, "Oh, do you have those, too?"

Ravenel spoke up in his best voice of authority. "See here, Mordred. Don't be a fool. Smuggling is one thing, but—"

"Quiet!" Mordred snarled, his thumb clumsily struggling with the hammer as he attempted to cock the pistol.

Ravenel prudently held his tongue. He could tell from Mordred's awkward handling of the weapon that he was a rank amateur, far more dangerous than a man who possessed any skill. If Ravenel could only contrive to knock the pistol aside, his and Gwenda's situation would not be entirely hopeless. He was confident he could handle Mordred and then there would only be the boy, Rob, and the one referred to as old Tom Quince.

While the baron assessed their chances, a rough voice called out, "Eh, what's happening here, Mordred?"

A hulking figure lumbered out of the shadows to stand beside the innkeeper. Ravenel's hopes plummeted at his first view of "old" Tom. Quince was a giant of man with coarse skin, a broad crooked nose, and a thatch of salt-and-pepper hair.

"Nothing's amiss. I can handle it," Mordred

said, although fine beads of sweat had broken out on his brow. "Just finish unloading those casks and get out of here before anyone else sees you."

Tom Quince did not appear in the least perturbed by this surly command. His eyes traveled contemptuously over Ravenel, taking in his brocade dressing gown.

"Flash cove." He sniffed. Then his gaze moved to where Gwenda knelt on the stable floor, her arms clutched around Bert's neck. The dog's tongue hung out, his bark issuing in a foolish-sounding grr-uff.

A sudden gleam sparked in Tom Quince's eye, which the baron much misliked. The smuggler's mouth split in a gap-toothed leer.

"If this be not Tom Quince's lucky day." The burly man licked his lips. "What a prime bit o' goods. Just what I've been hankerin' fer."

Ravenel saw his own dread mirrored in Gwenda's terrified eyes. He shouted at Quince, "You lay one hand on her, and by God, you'll regret it." He started toward Quince, forgetting the weapon trained upon him.

"You! S-stay where you are," Mordred said, the pistol trembling in his hand.

"I allers wanted me a fancy coachin' dog like that 'un." Quince hunkered down and proceeded to scratch Bert behind his ear.

So certain had Ravenel been that Gwenda was about to be ravished by this great brute, it took him several seconds to realize it was the dog Quince desired and not her.

Gwenda smacked the smuggler's hand away

from Bert. Dragging the dog with her, she inched farther back into the stall. "N-no. You leave Bertie alone."

"Quince, you damn fool," Mordred cried. "What are you doing? Forget about that cur before you queer everything."

But Quince ignored him, continuing to advance on Gwenda. "Now, little lady, don't raise a fuss. Old Tom ain't goin' to hurt you. Just be a good gel and give me the nice doggie."

"No!" Gwenda crouched back, her eyes turning in desperate appeal to the baron.

There had been times during the past two days when Ravenel thought he would have gladly surrendered Spotted Bert to the devil himself and said good riddance. But he took one look at the tears spilling down Gwenda's cheeks and an unexpected rage surged through him.

He plunged in between her and the smuggler, driving his fist into Quince's stomach.

"Stop before I fire," Mordred warned, taking aim.

Although Quince bent over and grunted, Ravenel's blow hardly seemed to affect the large man. He neatly blocked Ravenel's next punch, a toothy grin spreading over his face. "Oho, would you look at this struttin' gamecock? So it's a mill ye're after, laddie? Fine wit me. Ain't been no trouble wit the excisemen of late. Gettin' a mite dull. Want to fight me for the dog?"

"Be only too happy to oblige," Ravenel grated.

"Are you mad, Quince?" Mordred stepped forward with the pistol trying to take charge, but Quince jostled him aside.

"Ah, shut yer bone box. I got to show this fancy gent'mun here the proper way to throw a punch."

Before Gwenda's stunned senses could even register what was happening, Ravenel had stormed from the stable with Quince, Mordred trailing behind, still grumbling. Gwenda settled her bleary-eyed dog back down into the straw and got to her feet, scrambling after the men.

When she emerged through the stable doors, she saw Quince in the middle of the yard, yanking off his coat. He spit on both his palms and doubled up his fists. The baron quickly rid himself of his brocade dressing gown, stripping down to his breeches. Moonlight skated off the hard contours of his chest and arms as he assumed the fighter's stance.

Gwenda could only gape at his lordship in horrified astonishment. Merciful heavens! What the devil had gotten into the man?

"Ravenel!" she shrieked. But her outcry proved a mistake. By distracting his lordship, she enabled Quince to land the first blow. He caught Ravenel square in the eye, sending him flying backward into the mud.

Gwenda winced and started to run to him, but Ravenel was already jerking to his feet. He charged forward and got off a solid punch at his opponent's nose, succeeding in drawing his cork.

Quince gave a snort of surprise, then the fight commenced in earnest, blows flying left and right, both of them slipping and sliding in the mud. Gwenda stuffed her hand against her mouth, fearful of crying out again and breaking the baron's concentration. She sucked in her breath each time Quince's meaty fist connected with Ravenel's flesh.

Completely forgetting they were on opposite sides, Gwenda turned indignantly to Mordred. "Don't just stand there. Make them stop."

"I would if I could get off a clear shot," Mordred blustered. "Don't know why they're fighting over that vicious brute, anyway. Just look what he did to my leg."

But he got scant sympathy from Gwenda. She wrung her hands and thought of rushing in between the two men, but they were like a pair of raging bulls. Never had she seen Ravenel look so wild, a nigh savage light in his eyes, the sweat glistening on his muscular chest. His breath was coming hard; his knuckles were raw and bleeding. Yet Gwenda had the strangest notion that he was somehow actually enjoying this horrid contest.

So desperate was she that Gwenda began to think of rushing back to the inn to retrieve her pistol and rouse Jarvis, when she saw Quince waver slightly. Ravenel's next blow dropped the big man to his knees. Although his own chest was heaving, Ravenel yet held his pose waiting for Quince to get up.

The man turned his head to one side and spit out a tooth. He flung up on hand and gasped. "E-enuff."

Gwenda expelled her breath in a tremulous sigh, not quite trusting this capitulation. But the smuggler staggered to his feet, his split lip twisting into a lopsided grin as he held out one callused palm.

"Here. My hand on it. Never thought to see the day one o' the gentry could match Tom Quince. A pity ye be a lord, so it is. What ye might have done in the ring."

Gwenda watched in mute astonishment as the baron slowly shook hands with the smuggler and then Quince was pressing a flask of brandy upon him.

"Enough of this nonsense," Mordred shouted, marching forward and waving his pistol at Ravenel. "I want him locked up in the stable before he gets loose and fetches the excisemen—"

"His Nibs would never do that. 'E's a gent'mun. Somethin' you know nothin' about," Quince said loftily. "Now give me that 'ere afore you hurt someone." With that, he wrenched the pistol away from the abashed Mordred and tucked it into his own belt.

The entire scene grew hazy before Gwenda's eyes. As her disordered senses took in the fact that the fight was indeed over and it seemed that Ravenel had won, she felt nigh giddy with relief. She swayed on her feet, as close to fainting as she ever had been in her life.

Then a strong hand closed upon her shoulder, steadying her.

"Gwenda! Gwenda, are you all right?" Ravenel's deep voice sounded close to her ear. Someone pressed a flask to her lips, forcing a fiery liquid down her throat.

She sputtered and choked on the brandy, but the light-headedness left her. Her world snapped back into focus. Her gaze traveled up to Ravenel's face. His brow was furrowed with concern.

His cheek was turning purple, one eye was almost swollen shut, and he was asking *her* if she was all right.

"Oh, R-Ravenel!" she said, her breath catching on a sob.

Quince regarded her with pained surprise as he recorked his brandy flask. "Here now, there be no need to start a-snifflin' again. Tom Quince allus honors his word. You get to keep your dog. You can thank your man there for that. He certainly strips to advantage."

"I—I know." Some of the color flooded back into Gwenda's pale cheeks. "I—I mean I do . . . I—"

At that moment, the moon drifted from behind the clouds, illuminating her expression. Her gaze met Ravenel's, her green-gold eyes shining soft with gratitude and admiration.

It was most strange, Ravenel thought, staring back at her, suddenly conscious of being half-naked, his breeches mud-stained, his face battered. But for the first time in his life, Desmond Arthur Gordon Treverly could imagine what it was like to be a dashing knight, garbed in a silver coat of mail shining bright as the sun.

# Chapter 8

The late-afternoon sun charted a downward course by the time Ravenel spotted the rooftops of what had once been the sleepy fishing village of Brighthelmston, now a bustling fashionable resort owing to the Prince Regent's patronage.

His lordship slapped down on the reins of the hired tilbury, but the gray mare pulling the carriage set its own pace regardless. He did not attempt to urge the horse again and settled lazily back against the seat. He was not in a hurry for once.

"Brighton, Miss Vickers," Ravenel said, drawing in a deep breath, already scenting the salty tang of sea air. "I do believe we might make it this time."

His remark coaxed only a brief smile from Gwenda. She had been quiet and unusually solemn ever since they had set out from the Nonesuch at noon. Ravenel dragged his gaze from the road winding ahead and regarded her rather anxiously. He didn't care at all for the deep shadows under her eyes. She appeared like some pale waif garbed in that overlarge frock that belonged to Mordred's wife. Although he had to admit the green shade was becoming to her eyes, they seemed so lackluster. And he could wish for a little more color in her cheeks.

The baron trusted that a good sleep would restore her to her irrepressible self again. Goodness knows neither of them had gotten much of that last night. The only one who seemed unaffected by the previous eve's events was Bert. The dog wedged himself in between Ravenel and Gwenda, making a nuisance of himself by thrusting his head into Ravenel's line of vision and barking to be let down for a run. He appeared none the worse for the amount of brandy he had lapped up.

I should have such a hard head, the baron thought wryly.

When he was obliged to shift over on the seat to make more room for Bert, Ravenel winced. Damn! Was there any part of his anatomy that was not bruised from Quince's fists?

His lips parted in a rather painful smile. What a glorious fight it had been! The sparring he enjoyed at Gentleman Jackson's seemed staid by comparison, he mused, yet marveling at his own recent behavior.

In the early hours of the morning, he had recounted every detail of the fight with almost boyish enthusiasm to Jarvis. The old man ought to have been appalled to discover that his master had been brawling in the mud with a smuggler, then staying to tipple brandy with the rogue. But there had been a certain indulgence in Jarvis's manner, merely adjuring Ravenel to hold still as he had applied beefsteak to the swollen eye.

Not even as a lad had the baron ever so forgotten himself as to engage in boisterous wrestling or bouts of fisticuffs like his school fellows or cousins frequently did. Always he had been conscious that such ungentlemanly conduct was beneath the dignity of the Baron Ravenel.

Then what had become of his dignity in the stableyard of the Nonesuch? Ravenel still didn't know. Some ages-old constraint inside him seemed to have snapped, and he had made up for all the mischief denied him in his lost boyhood in a single night. Stranger still, he harbored no remorse, no self-recriminations at his lapse of reason. If anything, he felt amused recalling the episode with Tom Quince. When the man's wagon had finally been unloaded, the baron had shaken the smuggler's hand as though parting with an old friend.

And Mordred . . . Ravenel chuckled to himself at the memory, stopping abruptly at the twinge of pain in his sore jaw. Mordred had fallen over himself to be obliging, frightened that the baron might decide to hand him over to the authorities. Besides turning up with the gown for Gwenda, the innkeeper had offered his coach to convey Jarvis and the baggage to Ravenel's lodgings in Brighton. By some magic the host had also produced a tilbury for Ravenel to drive Gwenda home in, all this without asking for a single shilling in payment. Always eager to help a fellow creature in need, Mordred had crooned, and surely his lordship was not the man to hold a grudge against a poor innkeeper? So much for Gwenda's desperate, murderous villain. The baron wondered what she would say if he told her that he had discovered later that the man's pistol had not even been loaded.

He stole a speculative glance at his companion but could scarce see her face. Her head drooped forward, her bonnet and curls shading her eyes. She truly was exhausted, he thought, wishing he could draw her head down onto his shoulder. She had fallen asleep in such an awkward position.

But Gwenda was not asleep. She suffered not so much from exhaustion as from a severe attack of guilt. She could scarce bring herself to meet Ravenel's gaze all morning, astonished that he appeared so cheerful, what with those shocking bruises on his cheek, to say nothing of his poor eye.

It was all her fault. If she had listened to him and returned to her room, not dragged him out into the night looking for Bert, none of last night's escapade would ever have occurred. She had expected Ravenel to deliver a lecture that would last all the way to her parents' doorstep or at least to put on his martyred look.

How utterly unfeeling of the man that he chose to do neither! Here she was in the throes of remorse, willing, nay eager, to listen to a scolding in noble silence, and what must Ravenel do but sit there, looking so confoundedly nonchalant.

With the exception of his shocking black eye, he was rigged out in his usual manner, with stiff-starched cravat, somber-colored waistcoat and breeches, his curly-brimmed beaver perched upon waves of neatly combed ebony hair. But his behavior was most ... most un-Ravenel-like. The man acted as though he had not a care in the world but to enjoy the drive, the brightness of the day after last evening's storm. Why, at the moment, he was even softly whistling some tuneless ditty.

Unfortunately, Gwenda could think of only one way to account for his uplifted spirits. He had to be rejoicing in the knowledge that he was soon to be rid of her. Not that she could blame him, but the notion only added to her misery. Had she not brought disaster to him, from the moment she had thrust herself upon his notice at the White Hart, attempting to meddle in his relations with Miss Carruthers and involving him with stolen phaetons, chewed boots, coaching wrecks, treks through rainstorms and smugglers? Everything Ravenel had ever said about her was correct, Gwenda thought with a heavy sigh. Shatter-brained, heedless, impractical ... And to climax everything, he had been obliged to engage in a vulgar brawl to save her dog. Gwenda was certain that was an affront to his dignity that the baron would never forget.

She quickly blinked back the tear that threatened to trickle down her cheek. At least one good thing had come out of it all. The baron obviously had given over his foolish notion that he had to marry her. He had not mentioned it once this morning. Last night's affair must have brought him to his senses. Not even his lordship's rigid code of honor would require such a sacrifice, that he should tie himself to a female absurd enough to run abroad in her nightgown and become entangled with smugglers, a woman so sadly wanting in the sort of propriety and good sense Ravenel would demand of his wife.

She was glad of this, Gwenda told herself stoutly, for of course it was not as if she wanted to marry him. Just because the man did at times appear in her dreams as Roderigo, she certainly hadn't been so foolish as to fall in love with him. No, how utterly absurd that would be.

The tilbury gave a sudden jolt, which forced Gwenda to sit erect and clutch the side of the carriage. She realized with a start that they were rattling over the cobbled streets of the town itself and only his lordship's expert handling of the reins had prevented their locking wheels with a phaeton driven by some reckless young buck.

Even this did not serve to ruffle Ravenel's temper. With some amusement, he pointed out to Gwenda the distant outline of the Regent's whimsical pavilion. She eyed with little interest the classical villa with its central rotunda encircled by six Ionic columns. Beyond that a glass dome topped what was surely the most lavish structure ever built to stable horses. But the sight of the palace only served as a melancholy reminder to Gwenda that she and Ravenel were approaching the end of their journey.

All too soon the tilbury jounced along the Marine Parade toward that fashionable area of Brighton known as the Royal Crescent. The town house her family had rented proved to be one of the newer ones with charming wrought-iron balconies and canopied bow windows. The walls were glazed with black tiles to withstand the gales and salt spray of the sea.

As Ravenel reined in the shuffling gray mare, Gwenda prepared to jump down before his lordship could come around to assist her.

"I have given you enough trouble," she said primly. "But before we say farewell, I must tell you how much I . . . how truly grateful—"

"There's no need to go into that now. I am coming in with you." His lordship leaped somewhat gingerly from the carriage, wincing as he held a hand to his ribs. Bertie bolted right after him.

When Ravenel came around to hand her down, Gwenda shrank back. "Oh, n-no. I know how tired . . . how eager you must be to get to your own house. There is not the least necessity for you to come in with me."

"Indeed there is. I have to speak to your father."

Gwenda's eyes widened in dismay. "About what?"

" 'Tis customary to consult a lady's father in these delicate affairs. I need to assure him that I am going to marry you."

So Ravenel's mind had not altered. He was still insisting that she be his wife. A curious sensation of gladness stirred inside Gwenda, but she quickly suppressed it, recalling Ravenel's reason for doing so.

She answered rather sharply. "I told you you are not obliged to do that. I am willing to risk my reputation rather than enter into such—such an undesirable union."

For a moment, she fancied she saw a shading of hurt in his dark eyes, a pain that had naught

189

to do with his bruised flesh. "I had rather hoped you were starting to reconsider—" He broke off. "Never mind. I know what is proper. If you won't be sensible, I would as lief refer the matter to your father's judgment."

His cheerful manner vanished as he squared his jaw in a stubborn manner. He reached up, his hands spanning her waist. He lifted her rather forcefully from the tilbury so that she tumbled against him.

Gwenda quickly pulled herself back from the all-too-welcome support of his strong arms. " 'Tis you who won't be sensible. You have made your chivalrous offer; I have refused it. You ought to be satisfied."

"I won't be satisfied until I have talked to Lord Vickers."

Gwenda started to argue, but it was difficult to do so while fighting an unaccountable urge to burst into tears.

"Very well," she said. "If there is no other way to appease your infernal conscience! But I know full well how Papa will handle the matter."

Gwenda flounced away from him. While Ravenel consigned the horse and tilbury to the care of a groom, she marched up the town-house steps with Bert frisking alongside, swatting at her skirts with his tail.

The baron joined her at the door, his expression a mingling of obstinacy and trepidation. He might well have been a visitor contemplating his first excursion inside Bedlam, reluctant but manfully determined to face the ordeal ahead.

Knowing the contempt in which Ravenel held

her family, Gwenda anticipated the forthcoming introductions with dread. Lord knows, she was not ashamed of her family, but at times they could be so—so *enthusiastic* and Ravenel so stiff-necked.

She thought again of trying to turn him aside from his purpose, but the oak portal was already being swung open by a servant whose familiar tanned features seemed out of place in butler's garb.

"F-Fitch!" Gwenda gasped in utter astonishment.

"Miss Gwenda," the coachman exclaimed. "Praise the Lord!"

She could only stare at him, recalling that the last time she had seen the man Ravenel had been stuffing his unconscious form inside the coach.

"Fitch, what are you doing here?"

"The master gave over trying to make a coachman of me. He said I should try butlering—"

"No," the baron interrupted, looking equally astounded. "She means, how the deuce did you get here ahead of us?"

"Ah, Master Jack found me and James and fetched us here late last night." Fitch stepped back to allow Gwenda and Ravenel to enter the foyer. Before Gwenda could demand any further details from her erstwhile coachman, another male voice called out, "Fitch. Who is it?"

Gwenda tipped back her head, her gaze traveling up the marble staircase to the regions above. A youth attired in scarlet regimentals leaned over the gilt railing. So dashing, so manly did he appear in uniform that it took Gwenda a second to recognize her scapegrace brother until Jack's face lit up at the sight of her.

"Gwenda, you madcap!" He tore down the steps at such a rate he appeared certain to fall and break his neck.

"Oh, Jack! Jack!" With a glad outcry, Gwenda flung herself into his arms, momentarily forgetting everything but her joy in being reunited with her favorite brother.

They hugged while Bert leaped up at them barking, then both began to talk breathlessly, scarce giving the other a chance to reply.

"Damme, Gwen. Father's had me searching all over Kent for you . . ."

"Oh, I'm so sorry if I've worried everyone."

". . . and even after I found the wrecked carriage and that great looby Fitch, he had no notion where you'd got to—"

"I've been quite safe. But, Jack! Your new uniform. You look so smart!"

" 'Tis nothing to cry about, for mercy sakes. You already appear enough of a fright. Where'd you get that hideous dress?"

While in the midst of these greetings, a door off to Gwenda's right opened and other familiar, well-loved voices were heard.

"Jack? Did I hear Bertie's bark?"

"Is that our Gwennie come back?"

The next instant a short, plump woman rustled forward. Dear Mama, her military-style spencer and skirt as ever neat and precise. And just behind her, Papa, his dreamy eyes already filling with tears of gladness. Gwenda had not a chance to utter a word before her parents swept down upon her, embracing her.

Lingering upon the threshold, his presence gone unnoticed, Ravenel shifted his feet, beginning to feel a trifle awkward. With some hesitation, he removed his hat and handed it to Fitch. Studying the trio surrounding Gwenda, he had no difficulty recognizing Lord Vickers. The man's leonine mane of silver hair was a familiar sight at the House of Lords. The woman with the lace cap and unruly curls, of course, had to be Gwenda's mother, Lady Vickers. And as incredible as it seemed, the jovial, harmless-looking lad must be the infamous Mad Jack.

Yet even without observing the Vickerses all together, Ravenel felt he would have instantly known the members of Gwenda's family. It was not so much a strong facial resemblance they shared as it was that exuberance of manner that was so much a part of Gwenda's charm; an unaffected display of warmth and affection that marked them all as belonging together.

The baron took a step backward, suddenly feeling like an intruder here. He was on the point of taking back his hat and slipping quietly away when a lull finally occurred in all the hugging and exclamations.

"My dear child," Lord Vickers said to Gwenda, blowing his nose into his linen handkerchief. "I thought you were dead."

"Stuff, my dear!" Lady Vickers exclaimed. "Why must you always be thinking people are dead? One cannot be five minutes late coming back from the dressmaker's without you working yourself into a fret."

" 'Twas more than five minutes." Her husband raised his hand with a dramatic flourish. "To have one's only daughter vanish from the face of the earth! To find naught but the wrecked remains of her coach—"

At this juncture, Fitch startled them all by bursting into a loud lament. "Oh, 'twas all my fault, sir. That accursed drink. You should turn me off without a character, so you should."

In his fit of remorse, Fitch twisted and crushed the brim of the baron's hat. But before Ravenel could rescue his much-abused headgear, the butler turned and stumbled off toward the servant's stairwell, taking Ravenel's hat with him.

"Fitch!" Lord Vickers called. "Oh, the poor fellow. Fitch!"

"Let him go, my dear," Lady Vickers said. " 'Tis best he retires below until he composes himself. One cannot have a hysterical butler answering one's door, can one?"

It took the startled Ravenel a moment to realize her ladyship had directed this last comment to him.

"Oh! Er . . . no, it would not do at all."

Lady Vickers nodded in approval. "Such a sensible man. So good of you to call. 'Tis always so delightful to receive unexpected visitors. . . . Who are you?"

Her ladyship's acknowledgment of Ravenel's presence had the effect of also turning her son's and husband's attention upon him. To Ravenel, it seemed he was facing a veritable sea of curious green-gold eyes. He had never before experienced any difficulty in pronouncing his own name, but he found himself stumbling over it.

Gwenda came to his rescue. She pushed her way to his side, looking a little nervous and breathless herself. "This—this is Lord Ravenel, Mama. He—he is the gentleman who has been looking after me and has rescued me several times and—and risked his life fighting with smugglers and all manner of brave things."

Ravenel felt his cheeks wash a dull red. He wished Gwenda would have given him a more ordinary sort of introduction. He started to disclaim, but the Vickerses were already upon him, pumping his hand with enthusiasm: Lady Vickers reiterating her conviction that he was a sensible man, Jack terming him a "brick," and Stanhope Vickers declaring what a pleasure it was to meet the preserver of his most beloved daughter.

"I am your only daughter, Papa," Gwenda reminded him.

"So you are, my pet. So you are." Stanhope Vickers clapped his hands together. "Well, Lord Ravenel. We must adjourn to the parlor at once, and you and Gwennie can regale us all with an accounting of your adventures. Prudence, my own, mayhap a spot of tea—"

"No, sir. Please," the baron said quickly before he found himself entirely carried away from the purpose of his visit. "If it would be at all convenient, I would like the favor of a few words with you . . . alone."

Lord Vickers's surprise seemed to spread to the

rest of his family, with the exception of Gwenda, who leveled a deep frown at Ravenel, which he steadfastly ignored.

"Why, certainly, sir," Lord Vickers said. "If that is what you wish."

"Oho! What mischief has Gwenda been about this time?" Jack Vickers called out gleefully.

"Be quiet, Jack," Lady Vickers said. She disconcerted the baron by offering him a glance of unexpected shrewdness as her eyes traveled from him to her blushing daughter. She briskly shooed her son toward the door. "I am very sure you have some business that requires your attention elsewhere. And as for Gwenda, she is all done in. She should go upstairs for a hot bath and liedown. I will send Colette—"

Her ladyship paused a moment to frown. "Oh, no, that is right. Fitch told us Colette has run off. So sadly unreliable, but she did speak French so prettily."

"Mama, please," Gwenda said as soon as she could get a word in. "I am not in the least tired. I should like to wait—"

But her mother swept her protests aside. "As your grandpapa the general always said, a soldier is of no use in battle unless she has had the proper rest."

Ravenel had no chance to so much as speak to Gwenda before her mother was marching her up the stairs, gently straightening her daughter's shoulders as they went. Gwenda shot one anxious glance back at him, her look half pleading, half indignant.

Damn it, Gwenda, Ravenel wanted to shout. I

am insisting upon this marriage for your own good.

Then he caught a glimpse of himself in the cheval glass mounted on the wall and saw that he looked every bit as tense as she did. He followed Lord Vickers into the study for what he feared was going to prove the most awkward interview of his life.

". . . and that is the whole of the matter. So you see why I must marry your daughter," Ravenel concluded.

"Dear me," Lord Vickers said. "You and Gwennie certainly have had a most unfortunate time of it."

Considering Lord Vickers's usual flair for the dramatic, the baron found this a rather surprising bit of understatement. He wondered if Gwenda's father had understood one word of all that he had just related.

Seated behind a desk littered with rumpled parchment, half-mended quill pens, and dripping inkwells, Lord Vickers rocked back in his leather-covered chair, bridging his fingertips beneath his chin. He shook his head and blessed his own soul several times.

"So do I have your permission to go ahead with the marriage banns?" Ravenel prodded.

"I don't quite know what to tell you, young man." A gentle frown creased Lord Vickers's long forehead. "Any practical considerations of my daughter's future, I usually leave to her mother. We had much better consult her."

Without waiting for Ravenel's agreement,

Lord Vickers snapped to his feet with surprising quickness. He strode to the door, flung it open, and called for his wife.

Very shortly, Prudence Vickers poked her head in the doorway, a pair of wire-rimmed spectacles perched on her nose. "What is it, my dear? Are you ready for your tea?"

"Not just yet, my love. It would seem Gwennie has gotten herself into some sort of a coil. Last night she and Lord Ravenel were stranded together at an inn . . . er, the Nonesuch. By the by, it sounds rather quaint. Remind me to stop over there the next time we are traveling through Kent."

"Certainly, my dear."

The baron bit back an impatient oath. "The point is, my lady, that your daughter was unchaperoned and—"

"And so Lord Ravenel feels he ought to marry our Gwen," Lord Vickers finished.

Lady Vickers studied Ravenel over the top of her spectacles. "Oh? Is that your only reason for wishing to do so?"

The baron squirmed uncomfortably. If he had any other reasons, he was not quite ready to examine them. "It seems to me reason enough."

"And Gwenda?" Lady Vickers asked. "Is she enthusiastic about this notion?"

"N-o-oo," Ravenel said reluctantly. "I admit that she is not. But under the circumstances—"

"Then under the circumstances, she had better not do it."

"That is your opinion, is it, my dearest heart?" her husband asked.

"Indeed it is. Stanhope, only consider. Gwenda has already betrothed herself twice and broken it off because the affection was found wanting. A third time and it could develop into a most disagreeable habit."

Lady Vickers gave Ravenel an amiable smile so very much like Gwenda's. "Thank you all the same for your offer, my lord, however misplaced it may have been. I am sure in all other respects you are a most sensible man. Now do forget all this, and hurry along for tea."

With that, her ladyship popped back out again. The baron rubbed the back of his neck, thinking ruefully that Lady Vickers was certainly her daughter's mother. He heaved a deep sigh and made one last attempt to reason with Lord Vickers.

"Sir, with all due respect, what you and your wife don't seem to understand is if this tale leaks out, your daughter will be ruined. Society may begin to say a deal of other things about Gwenda, things far less pleasant than whispers of broken engagements."

"Shall they?" Lord Vickers asked. "Well, I think it far more important not to force two delightful young people into a marriage neither wants rather than take heed of idle gossip."

Ravenel opened his mouth and closed it again. What was he to say in the face of such impracticality?

Lord Vickers smiled and continued, "Lady Vickers and I only want our daughter to be happy."

"But, my lord—"

"In truth, those who love Gwenda, who value her as they ought, would know she could never have done anything bad. The opinion of the rest of the world simply doesn't matter."

Ravenel could only stare at the man. This was utter folly. He knew it was and yet . . . There was a soft glow in Stanhope Vickers's eyes as he pronounced these words, and a quality to his voice infusing it with wisdom, a gentle, loving wisdom that made the baron's own notions of duty and propriety ring quite hollow.

Mayhap it was not the Vickerses who were the half-mad fools, but himself and the rest of the world. Ravenel ran one hand across his brow in confusion.

"There, there, young man." Lord Vickers patted him on the back. "You come along with me. Things always seem much clearer after one's had a cup of tea."

The fiery ball that was the sun poised on the verge of dipping below the sea, the ever-darkening waves frothed against the shore, and the twilight sky streaked with rosy ribands of sunset.

"Blast!" Gwenda hissed, letting fall the delicate organza curtain. She had only laid down upon the bed for a few minutes, never intending to fall asleep. What if Ravenel were already gone?

She stumbled to the French gilt wardrobe and found a simple white muslin gown, which she donned. Barely taking the time to tame her mop of curls, she flung an Indian shawl about her shoulders and raced out of her bedchamber.

She rushed to the gilt railing and was about to tear down the stairs when she noticed the tall, broad-shouldered figure pacing the hall below.

Ravenel. She breathed a tiny sigh of relief. So he had not already fled the Vickers household in horror. He appeared to have survived the talk with her father, although exactly what had passed between the two men Gwenda could not tell from Ravenel's expression. He looked neither relieved nor disgusted, merely thoughtful.

When Gwenda began to descend the stairs, he glanced up at her, his mouth tightening with a wry grimace. "You need not look so apprehensive, Gwenda. 'Tis all over."

Gwenda paused at the foot of the steps. "And?" she asked anxiously.

"Your father has convinced me you were right to refuse my offer. I have no intention of troubling you any further." He drew himself up stiffly and Gwenda thought she detected a flash of hurt in his eyes. For the first time, it occurred to her how she must have wounded Ravenel's pride.

She wished she could think of something soothing to say, but ended by blurting out, "Then why are you lingering here in the hall?"

"I was on the point of leaving." He gave an exasperated laugh. "But it seems that Fitch has misplaced my hat. Your family is tearing apart the servants' quarters looking for it."

Gwenda blushed with mortification. "Oh, Ravenel, I am so sorry—" she began, then stopped. "No, I am not. I am glad of it, for otherwise I should have missed you." She added accusingly,

"You were going to leave without saying good-bye."

"Of course I wasn't! That is . . ." He took a few steps away from her. "You were resting. I did not want to disturb you. Now you look . . ." He paused to glance back at her, a warmth coming into his eyes. Then he quickly averted his gaze. "Much better," he concluded.

Gwenda felt her blush deepen and she fretted the ends of her shawl. This was absurd, she thought, after all that she and Ravenel had been through together, for both of them to be behaving so shy and awkward now.

She cleared her throat, preparing to say what she had attempted to earlier in the tilbury. "My lord, I want you to know how grateful I am for everything—"

"Please! No speeches, my dear." A mischievous smile tipped Ravenel's lips, as devastatingly charming as it was unexpected. It was the way he had always been meant to smile, Gwenda thought sadly, not in that constrained manner she knew he would adopt as soon as he set foot out the door.

She tried to assume a cheerful manner. "Well, I daresay you will find yourself quite busy. All those business affairs you have had to neglect because of me and—and . . ." She faltered. "Miss Carruthers will likely be in Brighton soon."

"I suppose she will." The baron appeared to sober somewhat at the mention of Belinda's name, although he asked teasingly, "Any more advice for me, Miss Vickers?"

Gwenda started to speak, then firmly shook

her head. At that moment Jack came bursting into the hall, carrying Ravenel's hat.

"Fitch locked it down in the wine cellar!" Her brother rolled his eyes. "I am not certain how well he is going to serve as a butler, either."

Ravenel merely smiled as he took the curly-brimmed beaver from Jack. He asked Gwenda to express his thanks to her mother and father, then shook hands with Jack. Under her brother's curious eyes, Gwenda thought Ravenel would do the same with her. But when she offered him her hand, he carried it to his lips and pressed a fervent kiss upon her wrist. He turned and strode out the front door, without glancing back.

He had not taken five steps away from the house when he heard someone call his name.

"Ravenel?"

He turned quickly at the sound of Gwenda's voice. She stood silhouetted in the doorway, the simple white muslin accenting her curves. The breeze ruffled her soft curls, her ever-changeable eyes assuming the green luster of the sea.

"Yes?" he asked hopefully.

"I—I do have some advice." She drew in a deep breath. "I—I hope that sometimes you will remember to be just a little improper."

Ravenel playfully tipped his hat in acknowledgment of her words. She withdrew into the house, the door inching closed. As soon as she was gone, his smile faded. He grasped his hat, heading toward where one of Lord Vickers's grooms had brought around his tilbury.

The baron was somewhat amused to see Spotted Bert waiting there in the gathering dusk. The dog barked at his approach, charging forward and wagging his tail.

"What! Did you think I was going to leave without saying good-bye to you, either?"

He bent down to scratch Bert beneath the chin, but he found his gaze traveling past the dog to the sea, which was wide and mysterious, lapping against the shingled beach, so empty, so wretchedly lonely.

Ravenel jerked to his feet, saying sharply to the dog, "Damn it, Bert. What a fool I am! I didn't have to marry her. I wanted to. That's why I've been going on and on about duty, making such a pompous ass of myself. I'm in love with the woman."

He started purposefully back toward the house, only to halt again. He glanced down at Bert padding by his side. "But 'tis of no avail, is it? She doesn't want to marry me. There is no reason that she should."

He thought of his title, his twenty thousand pounds per annum, the vast cold manor in Leicestershire. He stared at the Vickers town house where the lamps were already being lit, the light glowing warmly beyond the panes of glass. Through the open window he could hear the sounds of singing, laughter.

"I don't really have anything to offer her, do I?" Ravenel murmured, his shoulders sagging.

He replaced his hat on his head and turned to go, pausing to pat the dog one last time. "You will look after her, though, won't you, Bert?"

The dog cocked his head to one side. Bert's only reply was a low, mournful whine.

# Chapter 9

Gwenda dipped her quill pen in the ink and scratched it laboriously across the page. For nearly a week she had been closeted in her room, seated at the small desk by her window overlooking the sea. If she ventured out at all, it was only for her brief visits to Donaldson's Lending Library. But *The Sepulchre of Castle Sorrow* had not advanced much beyond the first chapter.

> *The wind whistled past the velvet curtains. The candle flickered and went out in a hiss of smoke. Roderigo felt the chill of the grave pervade the castle walls, the stench of decaying flesh, crumbling bones, and the dark deed long forgotten—*

The last word trailed away in a smear of ink as Spotted Bert nudged his cold nose against Gwenda's elbow. He thrust his head in her lap, whining, rolling up his eyes in mournful fashion. "Bertie, please!" Gwenda forced the dog back.

205

"How am I ever to accomplish anything with you moping all over me?"

Her exuberant Bertie did not seem to be himself ever since their arrival in Brighton, the day that Rav—Feeling a small twinge in her own heart, she suppressed the thought. No, likely it was only that the sea air did not agree with Bert. She blotted the ink and reached for her pen once more.

> The shade of an ancient warrior rose up before him, its bloodstained visage awful to behold. "Roderigo!" quoth the ghost in dire accents, which would have caused a man of less fortitude than the young count to swoon. "Roderigo! Arise. The time hath come to address the wrongs done me by your family."
>
> Roderigo staggered back, flinging one hand across his noble brow. "Before tea!"

Gwenda flung down her pen in disgust and tore the parchment in two. The pieces joined the others that littered the soft carpet at her feet. She started to lean her aching head against her hands when Bert startled her by springing up. Thrusting his head through the open window, he gave a series of short, joyous barks.

She stood up herself to peer out. But she saw nothing in the stream of fashionable coaches, gigs, and phaetons making their way along the Marine Parade to have aroused such excitement in Bertie.

She was about to haul the dog back from the sill when she spied the tall man walking along the grassy enclosure, his features obscured as he bent forward to keep his curly-brimmed beaver from being snatched by the stiff breeze. Gwenda's heart quickened only to plummet with disappointment when the man doffed his hat to a passing carriage. Not glossy strands of ebony but only an unfamiliar dull brown.

Spotted Bert's barking faded to a chagrined whine.

"Oh, Bertie!" Gwenda snapped. But her vexation had little to do with the dog. "Go on. Get out of here. Find a cat to chase."

Although Bertie hung back, she managed to thrust him out her bedchamber door, then slammed it behind him. But she immediately felt ashamed for being so short-tempered with Bert. Truthfully, these past days, she had been as bad as the dog, ever hopeful of catching a glimpse of a cravat with a little too much starch, a swarthy-looking man constraining his hard-muscled form beneath the stiff garb of a most proper gentleman. Yet if Ravenel ever was abroad, enjoying the Brighton sunshine, he never passed by her window.

"Anyone would think I was in love with the man," Gwenda grumbled as she sat back down at her desk.

That thought had been occurring to her all too often of late, a most frightening, distressing thought. Romantic as it was in books, Gwenda did not care for the notion of pining away from unrequited passion. She would much rather have a love that was returned, so that she might be comfortable and happy.

With Ravenel, that was too much to hope for. By the end of their journey, he seemed to have learned to tolerate her, to even be civil to her family. But that was a far cry from the warmth of feeling Gwenda would require in her lover. She had not heard so much as a word from his lordship in the past week.

Gwenda reached for another sheet of paper, then sat staring at the blank vellum. This foolishness would pass, she assured herself. Had she not fancied herself in love twice before? She had been much younger then, barely seventeen that disastrous season. She could smile at her youthful self now, all those torrents of emotion, the conviction that her heart would be broken in two if she was not able to marry Jasper. She had survived that only to be equally certain she would go into a decline and perish if she did not become Marlon's bride.

She did not experience any such violent fancies about Ravenel, only the feeling that as each bright sun-kissed day passed without his presence, the summer sky seemed permanently washed in gray.

Gwenda thrust the sheet and ink pot away from her. She was doing no good here. She might as well round up Bertie and take him out for a walk. She retrieved her bone-handled parasol, then descended belowstairs, whistling for Bert. The lower floor of the house basked in the afternoon silence, except for the distant strains of Papa practicing at the pianoforte.

Fitch informed her that the master had already demanded Spotted Bert's eviction. The dog always howled when her father sang, so Fitch had been obliged to chase Bert outside.

But although she stood on the front steps and called, Bert seemed to have raced off out of earshot. Gwenda could not face the prospect of returning to her lonely room, so she opted to venture on her walk without the dog. Yet her listless footsteps got her not much farther than the seven-foot-tall statue of the Prince Regent mounted in front of the Royal Crescent. Disgraceful thing, Gwenda thought. The buff-colored stone had been eroded by sea squalls until one arm broke off. Most mistook it for a likeness of Nelson.

She leaned against it, poking the tip of her parasol in the grass. A party of ladies and gentlemen rattled along the Parade in their carriage, all of them laughing, apparently bent on some excursion of pleasure. Then Gwenda watched a family with a large brood of children go past, likely off for some sea bathing. Why did the rest of the world always seem to be having a wonderful time when one was at one's most miserable?

"Hallo there! Gwenda! "

The sound of her brother's voice snapped her head around toward the distant line of town houses. Jack bounded down the steps and raced toward the grassy enclosure, waving something.

He came up to her, panting with indignation. "That blasted dog of yours is moving on from boots to belts now."

He thrust a strap of chewed leather in her face.

Gwenda pushed it aside weakly, mumbling that she was sorry.

Her brother, obviously bracing himself for a heated exchange, snapped his mouth closed and blinked. "What? " he asked. "No 'Plague take you, Jack' or 'If you didn't leave belts lying around, Bertie couldn't get them, Jack'?"

"I am not in the humor for quarreling." Gwenda sidestepped her brother. She tried to open her parasol, but the breeze coming off the sea was a shade too brisk. Abandoning the effort, she trailed away from Jack, heading for the shingled beach.

Her brother caught up with her and fell into step. "You are not in much of a humor for anything since you came to Brighton. I never saw such moping, unless it was that silly dog of yours. 'Tis beginning to put me in the hips just watching the pair of you."

Jack scuffed the toe of his boot along the beach, sending up a spray of smooth, shiny pebbles. "As if I didn't already have enough to make me blue-deviled. Thorne is about to descend on us *and* Papa's cousins from Cheapside. They all want to see me before I leave to join my regiment."

"That's nice, Jack," Gwenda murmured.

He caught her by the elbow, swinging her about. "I say, Gwenda. I've got a notion. Why don't you come to watch the military review on the Bluffs with me and my friend Neville Gilboys. He's a first-rate fellow. His family made him join the army, but he really wants to be a playwright. He's perishing to meet you and tell you all about this tragedy he means to write someday."

In her present mood, Gwenda shuddered at the thought of meeting an eager would-be writer.

But her brother persisted. "Do come! Neville's devilish handsome. Just like that Roderigo chap you're always dreaming about with blond hair and a trim mustache—"

"Roderigo doesn't have a mustache. He has ebony hair and dark eyes." Dark as the sea at midnight, Gwenda added to herself. Hugging her skirts close against the wind, she stared forlornly at the waves breaking over the shore.

Jack vented his breath in a frustrated sigh. "What's amiss with you, Gwen? I've never seen you like this before."

When she didn't answer, he planted himself in front of her. "I won't go away until you tell me." He injected that cajoling note into his voice that only he knew how to use so well. He always managed to wheedle her secrets out of her, and Gwenda knew she would be given no peace until she confided in him.

"I—I think I have fallen in love," she said.

"Not again!"

Gwenda did not appreciate his brotherly frankness, not when she had just bared her soul to him. "If you are going to take that attitude . . ." She began to walk back up the beach, but he caught her, forcing her to halt.

"No, no, Gwen. I am sorry. Come back. Who are you in love with this—" He amended hastily. "I mean, who is the lucky devil?"

She tried to maintain a stubborn silence, but

instead she found herself resting her head against Jack's shoulder, tears beclouding her eyes. "Lord Ravenel," she whispered.

"Ravenel!" Jack croaked, although he patted her back.

Gwenda straightened immediately, her cheeks firing with indignation. "Aye! Why did you pronounce his name in that odious manner?"

"I—I didn't mean anything by it. 'Tis just that he does not seem in your usual line, Gwen. Although he behaved splendidly fighting that smuggler for Bert, his lordship is not the most dashing sort." Jack hesitated, then blurted out, "In fact, there is rather something about him that reminds me of Thorne."

"Ravenel is not in the least like Thorne!" Gwenda bristled, then remembered that she had once told the baron the same thing. "Well, mayhap only a very little at times. But Thorne would feel quite self-righteous if one got hurt doing something wrong. Ravenel *is* the sort of man who, if I accidentally set the house on fire, would give me a blistering scold. But first he would make sure I hadn't been burned."

"I see," Jack said, then infused his voice with a generous enthusiasm. "Of course. The very sort of thing to make a girl dote upon a chap."

"You don't see at all." Gwenda shifted her gaze to the sea as though somewhere on the bright sparkling waters she would find the words to explain it to him. "Beneath his starched cravat, Ravenel *is* dashing. When I have dreams about Roderigo now, 'tis always Ravenel that I see coming through the mist. He has the most handsome eyes and when he ki—" She broke off, heat rushing through her at the memory. She stumbled on. " 'Tis not any grand gesture that makes him heroic, but all manner of foolish little things like—like tucking his coat around my shoulders in the rainstorm even when he was angry, and saving Bert even after Bert had chewed up his boot, and asking me if I was unharmed after his own head had nearly been broken by Quince's fist."

"You must be in love." Jack nodded solemnly. "You are not making any sense. If you care so much for him, why did you let Papa send him away when he had offered for you? "

"He does not love me." Gwenda sniffed. "There is someone else. Not that I believe he is in love with Miss Carruthers, either, but she is so much more proper than—"

"Belinda Carruthers? " Jack interrupted.

"Aye. Have you met her? "

"No, but I know *of* her. I ran into old Huddersby at the Ship Tavern just yesterday. Poor fellow was badly cut up; lost a big wager. It seems he had bet this Carruthers chit would wed the Earl of Smardon, but the earl didn't come up to scratch."

"And now I suppose Belinda will be only too pleased to receive Ravenel's addresses." Gwenda flushed with anger. "She has treated him so shabbily, keeping him dangling, telling him she is recovering from a broken heart. Some tale of being in mourning over a . . . a"—Gwenda searched her memory for the name Belinda had mentioned that day—"a Colonel Percival Adams of the Tenth Cavalry."

"The Tenth?" Jack said. "That's Neville's regiment."

Gwenda scarce heeded him as she added bitterly, "Somehow I never believed a word of what she said."

"Then, my dear sister, the thing to do is to eliminate this unworthy Miss Carruthers as a rival."

Gwenda slowly shook her head. She was not sure that Ravenel would care how sly Belinda was, merely that she would know the correct way to conduct herself as the future Lady Ravenel. Even without Belinda, Ravenel would not willingly consider Gwenda for that role. What had his lordship called her once? "The mistress of disaster."

Her shoulders sagged, her eyes once more filling with tears. This conversation with Jack had only succeeded in lowering her spirits. Debating the matter with her brother had done naught but to convince her how very much she was in love with Ravenel, and how hopeless it all was.

"It was most kind of you to listen, Jack," she said. "But there is naught to be done. I—I assure you I will recover." This time she turned and hurried back to the house, not giving him a chance to overtake her.

As Jack Vickers watched his sister racing along the beach, he made no effort to follow. She would recover, Gwenda had declared, but her brother was not so sure. He had never seen that kind of dull pain in her sparkling eyes before, a heartbreakingly wistful kind of despair.

"Damme!" he muttered. "How can I just march off to enjoy myself shooting Frenchmen, leaving poor Gwen in such a state? My only sister, after all."

Thoughtfully he walked along the sands, letting the water froth to the very tip of his boots. But the somber mood didn't last long. His spirits were as ebullient as the waves. Mad Jack Vickers never accepted any cause as hopeless. There was always *something* to be done.

# Chapter 10

Donaldson's Lending Library was a gathering place for the haut *ton* that flocked to Brighton for the summer: a place to hear the latest gossip, to play at cards, to try out some new sheet music upon the piano forte—in brief, to do anything but select a book to read. Or so it seemed to Gwenda.

She irritably brushed past the group of ladies crowded upon the veranda, smoothing out their light muslins, chattering about how positively dowdy Mrs. Fitzherbert had looked while attending the theater last night.

Inside the library itself was no better. To even reach the book stacks, Gwenda first had to skirt by three dandies studying copies of the latest caricatures by Gilray through their quizzing glasses.

"Dashed amusing, 'pon my soul," one of them drawled. "Depicting that rascal Bonaparte as a pygmy. What will Gilray think of next?"

The dandy's voice sounded oddly familiar to Gwenda. She angled a glance from the corner of her eye and was horrified to recognize the Honorable Frederic Skeffington, the man who had accosted her in the inn yard of the Dorset Arms. Mindful of Ravenel's admonishment that Skeffington was a "loose screw," Gwenda for once behaved in a prudent fashion. She ducked behind one of the bookshelves before Skeffington spotted her yet again without any female chaperone.

While waiting for the three gentlemen to move on, she feigned to examine Volume Four of the latest edition of the *Encyclopaedia Britannica*, never intending to eavesdrop on the conversation. But when she overheard one of them mention Ravenel's name, her heart skipped a beat and she could not help listening more intently.

"Yaa-ss, Sobersides Ravenel has been behaving in a damned odd manner of late." There was a pause, then a loud sniff. Gwenda realized that the speaker had stopped to take a pinch of snuff and waited in an agony of impatience for him to continue.

"Met him along the Steine the other day when me and Froggy Blaine were comparing times of our last run to Brighton. Did it in four hours, fifty-two minutes, I said. Then I asked Ravenel most civilly how long it had taken him. 'Three days,' said he, and broke into hysterical laughter."

Gwenda bit back a rueful smile of her own, but she heard Skeffington and the other man exclaiming in shock.

"Sobersides? Laughing?"

" 'Pon my word, who would have thought it?"

"And there is worse," the first man said. "I chanced to make some little jest about that old fool Stanhope Vickers and Ravenel glowered at me like a mad dog. Said if I had half as much wit as Lord Vickers, I might know when to keep my mouth shut."

Gwenda, as astounded as the others to hear this, dropped the encyclopedia volume on her toe. Stifling an outcry of pain, she bent to retrieve it. It might well have been Skeffington's other friend who had been struck, however, for the man gave a low moan.

"That tears it, then. I was one of the few who wagered Belinda Carruthers would have Sobersides in the end. But if Ravenel is going to start acting as queer as Dick's hat band . . ."

"Your chances have been quite scotched in any case, old boy." Skeffington spoke up. "I happened upon Ravenel myself while traveling to Brighton last week. He was in the company of some pretty little thing making the journey with her aunt. When I uttered a few pleasantries to the lady, he behaved very much like a jealous lover. Nearly gave me a leveler."

Skeffington's companions gasped.

"Dear me!"

"Extraordinary!"

Gwenda thought so herself, and the book nearly slipped from her grasp a second time. Ravenel, a jealous lover? She had never considered his actions in that light. But she immediately quashed the tiny flicker of hope, telling herself Freddie Skeffington was a great dolt.

She leaned up against the bookshelf, waiting anxiously to hear what else might be said. The three men had fallen so quiet, she began to wonder if they had moved on. She peeked cautiously around the side, then choked back a small outcry as she saw the reason for the dandies' sudden silence.

The object of their conversation himself had just walked through the library door, Belinda Carruthers draped upon his arm. Gwenda's pulses gave a leap, part joy, part dismay, as her hungry gaze drank in the sight of Ravenel. Every detail of him, from the broad outline of his shoulders to that overstarched collar, from the brilliant dark eyes to the stubborn line of his jaw, seemed so inexpressibly familiar and dear to her heart.

She looked for some sign of the change in him that the dandies had been discussing, but she could detect nothing odd in Ravenel's manner. He stood as stiffly, as formally erect as ever. If anything, his reserve appeared more pronounced, his movements more perfunctory, as though he was not capable of taking pleasure in anything.

It hurt Gwenda to see that as much as it did to watch Belinda cling to Ravenel in that proprietary way. Gwenda swallowed the lump rising to her throat and shrank back behind the shelves.

The baron did not notice her skirts whisking from sight as he nodded his head in curt greeting to Freddy Skeffington and his two companions. They barely acknowledged it, smiling nervously and skittering by him as though he had the plague. Ravenel gave a slight shrug. Skeffington and his lot had always been a parcel of fools.

With great effort, Ravenel kept his gaze from sweeping about the rest of the library. He could not help telling himself that if there were any chance of encountering Gwenda in Brighton, it would most likely be here at the circulating library. But even if he chanced to see her again, what would that do but make him feel more empty and lonely than he already did?

"My lord?"

He felt Belinda tug at his sleeve and glanced down at her with some impatience.

"I would far rather have gone to the card assembly at the Old Ship. But since you insisted upon coming here, are you not going to at least select a book?"

There was a certain waspishness in Belinda's usually dulcet tones. As though she realized it herself, she was quick to flutter her eyelashes and add, "I know what a busy man you are. Indeed I was surprised and so flattered that you were able to spare the afternoon to escort me at all."

It would have been difficult to do anything else, Ravenel thought wryly. He had been deluged with missives from Belinda ever since her arrival in Brighton, assuring him that he was quite free to call upon her any time he wished.

As she flitted away from him to effuse greetings over some portly dowager and her freckle-faced daughters, Ravenel noted the high bloom in Belinda's cheeks. He thought sardonically how remarkable the sea air in Brighton must be for mending broken hearts. Belinda had never looked better and had not mentioned anything more about being in mourning. Perhaps the cure came less from the sea than from the tidings being bruited about that the Earl of Smardon had become engaged to his cousin.

Ravenel checked his cynical thoughts. In truth, he scarce gave a damn about any of it. While waiting for Belinda, he ran his fingers listlessly over some volumes arranged on a shelf, barely registering the titles until he came to one neatly tooled in red leather.

*The Castle of Montesadoria* by G. M. Vickers. Ravenel eased the book almost reverently off the shelf, then thumbed through the pages, one particular line catching his notice. His lips curved into a tender smile as he read, "The count was a gentleman of most noble mien with handsome dark eyes."

What a flood of memories those words unleased, memories that were sharply dispelled by the sound of Belinda's voice close by.

"Ravenel!"

The petite blonde peered past his shoulder and cooed, "What have you found that has you so absorbed?" When she saw the book, she broke into tinkling laughter. "My dear Ravenel, you surely don't read that sort of book?"

He glared at her, not feeling at all like "her dear Ravenel."

"What, pray, is wrong with this sort of book?"

"Why, 'tis the most arrant sort of rubbish about ghosts and—"

"Until you are clever enough to write one, you should not feel so free to criticize."

Belinda's violet eyes widened. She looked as taken aback by his rudeness as Ravenel was feeling himself. Coloring, she said, "Naturally I would never do anything so vulgar as to write for money." She added with a self-deprecating smile," Of course, I do dabble a little with poetry."

"I detest poetry." Ravenel closed the book with

a snap and replaced it on the shelf. What was amiss with him? It was as though he were deliberately trying to provoke a quarrel with Miss Carruthers.

Not that there appeared any likelihood of that. If Belinda was offended, she quickly concealed it behind a coaxing smile. She tucked her hand through his arm, gushing, "Much more pleasurable than any sort of literature is music. I do so dote on music. Let us see what new songs there are."

She swept over to the pianoforte, quickly sifting through the sheet music, asking for Ravenel's opinion of which she should try. She could have played "Rule Britannia" for all he cared. He scooped up one sheet and handed it to her, having no idea what he had selected as she arranged her skirts on the bench.

Belinda played well, or so most of society would judge, Ravenel mused. But he found her performance wanting in any spark of genuine feeling for the notes she thumped out with such precision. She knows nothing of—of *enthusiasm and dreams*, Ravenel thought, recalling Gwenda's words. Miss Carruthers appeared far more concerned with how well she looked seated at the instrument, tossing her golden curls, her dainty fingers rippling down the keys.

In that instant Ravenel knew he would never marry Miss Carruthers or any other society miss like her. His duty be hanged! He had cousins enough to make up for his own lack of heirs. He would spend the rest of his days at Ravenel, alone. On a cold winter's eve by the solitude of his hearth, he would take out the memory of three glorious days in his life spent in the company of a green-eyed wood sprite who both vexed and amazed and made every moment one of wondering surprise. The baron doubted that he would ever experience anything unexpected again.

This dismal thought had no sooner occurred to Ravenel when the door swung open, nearly slamming Freddy Skeffington against the wall. An officer in a cavalry uniform swaggered through the door.

"So sorry, old chap," he said, doffing his tricorne to the outraged dandy.

Freddy, prepared to sputter and take umbrage, stopped in midsentence, gaping at the soldier. Ravenel could not blame Skeffington. The colonel was a most extraordinary-looking individual. His hair appeared darkened with some strange substance that plastered it to his skull. A mustache of the same startling shade of black appeared shoved beneath his nose. His shoulders, which Ravenel could tell had been padded with buckram wadding, shifted, becoming uneven.

With a final nod to Freddy, the officer set some young ladies by the watercolor books to giggling when he paused to shoot them a killing glance. Ravenel had an odd feeling he had seen this person somewhere before. But surely he would have remembered anyone who looked that peculiar.

The soldier halted in midstep as he spied Miss Carruthers at the piano. He clasped one hand to his heart and strode over. "Belinda, my darling. It is you!"

Belinda's playing stumbled to an abrupt end. She stared up at the officer bending over her and

223

said in affronted accents, "Sir! I do not believe that I have the honor of—"

"Belinda, it is I. Percy!"

"P-Percy?" Miss Carruthers said faintly.

"Aye. Your lost love, Colonel Percival Adams, whom you believed killed in the wars."

"I . . . I . . ." Belinda shrank back, turning as white as her muslin gown. Ravenel, equally astonished, stared at this apparition supposedly returned from the dead. So this was Belinda's Colonel Adams, he thought with a shake of his head. He had never thought Miss Carruthers a brilliant woman, but he had given her credit for having some discernment.

"There—there must be some mistake," Miss Carruthers babbled.

"The only mistake, my dearest, was my taking so long to rush back to your side," the colonel declared. He seized Belinda's hands and planted a fervent kiss upon each of them, which had the effect of knocking his mustache slightly askew.

Peering closer to look beneath the soldier's downswept lashes, Ravenel glimpsed mischievous green-gold eyes. As the jolt of recognition flashed through him, his lordship straightened, groping frantically for his handkerchief. He doubled over, apparently seized by a fit of choking.

By this time most of the other occupants of the library realized that something strange was occurring. Some listened with their heads discreetly averted, while Skeffington and his cronies gawked shamelessly.

Yet huddled behind the encyclopedias, Gwenda wondered in despair if she would ever be able to escape without the pain and embarrassment of encountering Ravenel and Miss Carruthers again. At the last glance she had stolen, they had seemed rooted by the pianoforte for the remainder of the afternoon.

But it gradually became borne in upon her that the music had stopped, that the hum of conversation in the library had grown strangely quiet.

"No!" Miss Carruthers's shrill outcry split the air. "You stay away from me."

"Forgive my impulsiveness, Belinda, my darling," a man's upraised voice said, "but we have been separated for so long."

A most familiar man's voice, Gwenda thought, freezing. With a feeling of dread, she inched out from behind the books and stared toward the pianoforte.

It would have taken more than boot blacking in the hair and a false mustache for Gwenda not to have known her own brother. A soft groan escaped her as she watched Jack pursuing the frantic Miss Carruthers around the pianoforte where she sought to take refuge behind Ravenel.

"I've been a prisoner of the French. With amnesia," Jack declared. "But as soon as I got my memory back, I escaped and returned so that we could be married."

"I am not engaged to you! I have never been engaged to anyone," Belinda shrilled. "I don't even know any Colonel Percival Adams." She appealed desperately to Ravenel. "My lord, save me from this madman."

But Ravenel seemed strangely quiet, muffling his face behind his handkerchief.

Gwenda had no difficulty guessing what her brother was attempting to do. Her face heating scarlet with misery and humiliation, she rushed forward to stop him.

"Jack!" she said, jerking roughly at his arm.

Her brother paused in his pursuit of Miss Carruthers to glance down at her. He pulled a fierce face.

"You are mistaken, miss. I am Colonel Percival—"

"Stop it!" Gwenda choked. She reached up and wrenched off the false mustache.

"Ow!" Jack cried, clapping a hand to his upper lip. He eyed her reproachfully. "This would be the one day you'd decide to come out of your room—just in time to be here and ruin everything."

Gwenda turned brusquely away from him. She could not raise her eyes to face either Ravenel or Belinda. "M-Miss Carruthers. I—I am so sorry for what my brother—"

But she got no further, for Belinda expelled her breath in an angry hiss. "Then this has all been some sort of horrid prank at my expense." She whipped about, clutching at Ravenel. "My lord, I have been insulted. I demand you call this rogue out at once."

Up until this time, Ravenel had been trying most heroically to contain himself. But Belinda's final dramatic appeal put the finishing touch on this farce. The laughter erupted from his chest until tears blurred his eyes. His mirth spread quickly among many of the other library patrons who had been staring until the entire room seemed to ripple with laughter.

Belinda's face stained scarlet. She slapped Ravenel hard across the cheek with the full force of her palm. "You! You are as vulgar as that scoundrel."

Her venomous glare shifted toward Gwenda and her brother. "And—and as for the pair of you, you should both be flogged and never permitted near decent society again!"

She whirled on her heel and stormed from the library, nearly oversetting Frederic Skeffington, who had the misfortune to be lingering in the doorway.

Ravenel could not seem to stop laughing, even while rubbing his stinging flesh, until he focused on Gwenda's face. One sight of the tears streaking down her cheeks put an abrupt end to his merriment.

"How—how could you, Jack!" she whispered brokenly.

Jack Vickers crossed his arms over his chest, looking somewhat abashed but defiant. "What did you expect me to do? I couldn't let my only sister die of a broken heart. I thought if I could only get rid of that Carruthers wench . . ." Jack glanced earnestly at Ravenel. "My lord, surely you can see that you oughtn't to marry a lady who has already begun to tell you lies. I know my sister can be a bit of a nuisance at times, but at least she is honest and she loves—"

"Be quiet, Jack! I shall never confide in you again as long as I live." Gwenda's tear-dampened lashes swept up and for one moment Ravenel stared deep into her eyes so full of despair, so full of . . . yearning.

"Gwenda," he breathed.

But she was already fleeing from him, rushing toward the door of the library. This time Skeffington had the wit to dive for safety as Gwenda plunged past him.

Ravenel took several steps after her, then stopped, judging it best to let her go for the moment. His mind was yet reeling, wondering if what he had thought he had seen shimmering in her eyes could possibly be true. He turned back to confront her brother.

Jack nervously straightened the hem of his scarlet coat. "I—I think I'd just better be getting along myself." He gave the baron a brief salute and tried to inch past him.

But Ravenel caught him by the sleeve. "Not just yet, my dear Colonel Adams. You and I needs must have a little talk."

A heavy fog was rolling in from the sea, seeming to bring the summer's day to an early close. As Gwenda took Bertie for his evening walk along the beach, she wished she could simply be swallowed by the mist forever.

Still reliving in her mind the whole disastrous episode at Donaldson's that afternoon, she could think of no better fate than to be buried in the sands and have the tides wash over her head.

Jack had knelt outside her bedchamber door begging for forgiveness through the keyhole until Mama had finally made him go away and leave Gwenda alone. Gwenda tried to remind herself that Jack had acted out of deep affection for her, but if only he would stop to think before plunging into one of these outrageous schemes.

His bungling had only made her life ten times more miserable. Not only had he involved Lord Ravenel in the sort of public scene that she knew so well he detested, but with half of the *ton* looking on, Jack had blurted out to Ravenel that Gwenda was in love with him. Although she would pen his lordship a note of apology, she would never, never be able to face the man again.

Gwenda sniffed, then quickly wiped her eyes on her sleeve. One would think she'd be cried out after the amount of weeping she had done that afternoon. She took a deep breath and tried to derive some pleasure from the walk with Bertie. But, at the moment, even the sea looked cold and gray.

Bertie barked and leaped at her skirts as though attempting to cheer her. She picked up a piece of driftwood and flung it far down the beach for him to chase. He quickly plunged after it and scooped it into his mouth. But while Bertie might have learned to do that much, he could never quite grasp the fact that he was supposed to bring the stick back.

He tore off with it, expecting Gwenda to chase him. As her dog rapidly disappeared into the fog, Gwenda began to fear that mayhap throwing the stick had not been such a good idea. She was in no mood to play hide-and-seek.

"Bert!" she called. But the fog muffled her voice and she heard no answering bark. The thick salt spray of the sea seemed to hang in the air, chilling her. Gwenda wrapped her arms about herself, wishing she had remembered to wear a shawl. She walked on a little farther until she heard a noise. It was as though pebbles on the beach had been dislodged.

"Bertie?" She squinted, peering along the hazy shoreline. She thought she could just discern the outline of someone approaching. Too big to be a dog. It had to be . . . Gwenda tensed, her lips parting in apprehension. It had to be a man. . . .

Out of the mists he came, the sea breeze ruffling his midnight-dark hair, a black cape flowing off his broad shoulders.

Gwenda froze in her tracks, wondering if she was dreaming. She pinched her arm until she knew a great bruise had to be forming and yet the stalwart figure approached until he stood within an arm's reach of her trembling hand.

Ravenel. Gwenda could not even persuade her numbed lips to form his name. The only thing that prevented her from sinking to her knees was her noticing that he looked as gruffly shy and embarrassed as she.

"My dearest—" He broke off, ruefully raking his hand back through his hair. "Damme! I spent all afternoon trying to memorize that passage, and I still cannot remember how it goes."

"Passage?" Gwenda asked weakly, her mind struggling to grasp the fact that he truly was here and wearing a cape, a black cape with three tiers and a scarlet lining.

"The passage from your book. You see, Jack wasn't able to give me enough details about how the dream was supposed to proceed."

Gwenda wrenched her eyes from her wondering inspection of Ravenel's new cape. She did not even need to ask what dream. Jack might well be her favorite brother, but she was going to kill him.

Gwenda backed away from Ravenel, her throat constricting with misery. "Oh, n-no, you needn't try to . . . because Jack told you . . . and now you feel s-sorry for me. Th-that entire scene at Donaldson's—"

"Forget what happened at Donaldson's," Ravenel said huskily, taking a step closer. "You need to tell me what Roderigo usually says when he comes out of the mist."

"He—he never says anything. He just—" Gwenda's voice cracked and she was unable to continue.

"He does something. Something like this?"

Gwenda's heart pounded as the baron slipped his arms about her waist.

"Y-yes," she whispered. Her gaze came slowly up to meet his, the intensity in his night-dark eyes taking her breath away. He gathered her closer, molding her against the hard plane of his chest.

As Ravenel's mouth moved to claim her trembling lips, a familiar bark sounded out of the fog. Gwenda groaned softly as she heard her dog come bounding along the beach. As Ravenel drew back, hesitating, Gwenda saw Bertie leaping up on his hind legs, the driftwood in his mouth. For the first time in his life, Spotted Bert had decided he was going to come back with the stick.

Why now, Bertie? Gwenda could have groaned.

At the sight of Ravenel, the dog dropped the wood and gave a joyful bark. Ravenel cursed under his breath as Bertie launched himself at them, leaving a trail of wet sand along the baron's cape.

Ravenel released Gwenda as he struggled to restrain the exuberant dog. "Not now, Bertie, old chap," he said through gritted teeth.

"Th-throw the stick and he'll chase it," Gwenda advised.

Ravenel snatched up the driftwood and flung it away with all his strength. Bertie gave another excited bark and pelted after it, spraying pebbles as he disappeared back into the haze.

But the romantic moment was entirely spoiled. Gwenda shivered, rubbing her arms.

"Damnation, Gwenda," Ravenel scolded. "What are you doing out here without a shawl? Do you want to catch your death?"

He swept the magnificent cape off his own broad shoulders and began to wrap it around her.

Gwenda tried to resist. She forced a tremulous smile, saying, "No, Ravenel. Y-you really must not go about thinking 'tis your duty to look after every woman who falls in love with you."

"My duty be damned!" He swept her up in the cape and caught her hard against him, his lips crashing down upon hers in a fiery kiss that left her mind reeling, her knees feeling weak.

He drew back long enough to breath in a fierce whisper, "I love you, you little fool. Will you be my wife?"

It was the most wonderful proposal that Gwenda had ever heard. But she tried to retain enough good sense to protest. "You—you couldn't possibly mean that—"

He silenced her with another kiss, his lips

sending such a rush of heat through her veins that she had no more need of the cloak.

It was several long, blissful moments before he would permit her to speak again.

"Oh, Ravenel," she said, burying her face in the lee of his shoulder. "Are you certain? After all the terrible things I've done to you. The first day you ever met me, you—you lost your most prized horses—"

"That was the most fortunate day of my life." He pressed a number of kisses against her curls, the top of her brow. "I wish Dalton much joy of the wretched beasts."

Gwenda clearly saw there was no reasoning with a man whose mind was as far gone as that. She ceased to try, merely turning her face up so that Ravenel's lips could continue his feverish explorations. She waited breathlessly as he prepared to kiss her again, but he suddenly became solemn.

His mouth quirked into a sad half-smile. "I cannot entirely deceive you, Gwenda. I fear I will always be something of a . . . a sobersides, tempted to make speeches and lecture you—"

"Just as I will always be a little shatterbrained." She sighed. "And there is my family—"

"No. Your family is completely charming. I was a pompous ass to ever say otherwise."

"You won't find Thorne charming," Gwenda warned him, resting her forehead beneath Ravenel's chin. "Or the rest of Papa's cousins who have just gotten out of debtor's prison or the uncle who likes to keep his sheep in—"

But Ravenel laughed shakily and embraced her again, bringing an end to this daunting list.

233

Locked in each other's arms, they gave over trying to convince each other why they should not be married. He cupped her chin between his fingers and fiercely demanded her answer.

"So, will you marry me, or do you intend to condemn Jarvis and me to a lifetime of utter propriety?"

"Oh, no, I would never do that. I—I mean, yes, Ravenel, I will marry you."

The completely unrestrained smile of joy that he gave her caused Gwenda's heart to ache with loving him.

"My darling," he said, crushing her tightly against him, then added after a brief pause, "Under the circumstances, could you not begin to call me Desmond?"

"I could never call you that under any circumstances," Gwenda said firmly. Then she sighed. "Roderigo."

"Oh, no!" Ravenel shuddered. "Absolutely not."

"My love," Gwenda amended.

Since Lord Ravenel had no objection whatsoever to this manner of address, the pact was sealed with a kiss.

*The moon rose slowly in the night sky, its gentle white light parting the mists to shine softly upon three figures yet silhouetted by the sea . . . the lady Gwenda strolling by the side of her dark-haired lover. And, of course, her dog.*